"Overall, it is easy to get lost in these stories; sometimes I didn't want them to end. Each story is an escape to somewhere different and unknown, where there is some kind of discovery at the end. The stories have a depth and feeling to them that make them highly enjoyable. What I like most about many of the stories is that days after having read them the characters and the scenes are still with me."

-San Francisco Book Review

"More Carver than O. Henry, Gale's stories are less about intricate plots and surprise endings and more about insight and the beginning of understanding. He shows a keen eye for detail, both physical and emotional. His dialogue is true to his characters. His physical descriptions paint easily conjured pictures, and his prose is confident whether examining the wretched or the wistful. All in all, this young writer's collection marks an engaging beginning to a promising career."

-US Review of Books

The Stories
That Make Us

SHAWN GALE

To order additional copies of this book, contact:
Xlibris
1-888-795-4274
www.Xlibris.com
Orders@Xlibris.com
722315

Foreword

Throughout history, artists' motivations for the creation of art have varied. It's been done to entertain, educate, self-express, confer blessings, perform catharsis, gain spiritual fulfillment, or simply to share stories.

Whatever the motivation, I believe art ought to inspire thoughts and feelings and give rise to what may be, what could be. The stories in this collection do not have a unified theme, and the styles in which they are written are as radically different as their odd, imperfect characters. I will let you decide what they are saying.

The Stories That Make Us

Acknowledgments

I would like to thank Yvonne, Marvin and Madison.

You need chaos in your soul to give birth to a dancing star.
-Friedrich Nietzsche

Contents

Transactions for Love

She lived in an industrial area, pure utilitarian, on the outskirts of the outskirts of the city. There were no park benches under the shade of oaks and maples, no people reading books, newspapers, or tablets, or chatting or texting on phones. There were no parents wheeling children in strollers or children frolicking about chasing one another, nor were there any teenagers tossing Frisbees or punting hackie sacs or kicking soccer balls. There were no people walking dogs. There were no young or middle-aged couples or old couples whispering romantic promises while walking hand-in-hand.

For wildlife, Jess had only seen crows. They were always perched on the power lines and rooflines and fence tops, cawing, swooping down to yank worms that had managed to wriggle out of cracks in the asphalt. And since she moved into the flat at 555A Industrial Way last spring, she'd been watching—searching at times—for wildlife. The lack of it made her long for Bala and its abundance of robins and woodpeckers and whitetail deer and black bears and raccoons and porcupines. But it was more than that. It was the scent of spruce and pine. It was the summer tourists and of course the year-round locals. It was the cranberry marshes and copper-hued lakes full of bass and walleye and the forests' canopies that in a month from now would change to yellow, red, and orange. It was the pebbly-shored beaches she'd walked on barefoot for so many summers that the soles of her feet were like the bottom of cork sandals, and it was the mosquitoes and black flies she despised yet loved because they let her know she was at home.

In the beginning, she enjoyed living in the city and student life at Ryerson. She involved herself in a number of social groups that in their infancy were indomitable forces the way ideology groups were when led

1

by the young, confident, and passionate. After the G20 protests and ensuing arrests, the membership of the groups waned and the remaining members' enthusiasm faded until it seemed like there was not enough vitality to carry on the good fight. It was a lesson. An awakening. Jess had learned that lofty ideals were easily crushed by the all-mighty dollar, her university courses only reinforced that understanding. *Realpolitik*. A year and a half in, halfway to her degree, she questioned why she had chosen to pursue History with all the inextricable misery. Even what seemed to balance things out, like South Africa and Myanmar, were a sham.

Words like slavery, colonialism, displacement, self-determination, genocide, hegemony, imperialism, and nationalism all carried stories so cruel and savage and brutal that she thought *humankind* would be better off wiped from the history books, the dictionaries, the world's collective psyche. When she let her feelings be known, some said it was so we didn't allow it to happen again. But it always did happen. Again and again. It was cyclical and boiled down to greed. We want what you have so we will convert you into following our beliefs which will allow us to control and exploit you, or, we will send in our armies and conquer your land and crush your people and take everything. Democracy was synonymous with dictator, oil with affluence, globalization with exploitation, as any first-year History student could see as easily as the giant billboard for Trojan Ribbed Condoms down the road. Even women's suffrage and slave emancipation and the creation of the United Nations along with its interventions had failed to staunch the blood from the wounds we had spent centuries gouging and cutting open.

During her final semester, while she lay in bed and the wind tossed the curtain and cast shadows she tried to name, two armies began waging war inside of her. And months later at convocation, when her name was called, she stood and marched up to accept her diploma. She shook Dean Roger's hand and faked a smile and waved to her grandmother, then joined the other Ryerson alumni. At that moment, she knew which side had won.

She was now sitting in front of a blank pale-grey paper tacked to a wooden backboard, holding a red crayon limply in one hand and a glass of red wine tightly in the other. It was her third—the glass of wine—and almost empty. She knew Milan would show up in the morning for the rent, red-eyed and unshaven, probably reeking of vodka and cigars. A few weeks ago he'd shown up and slurred his words as he informed her that he was there to paint over the large yellow peace symbol "some hoodlum" had spray-painted with yellow paint on the driveway. Then he sung a folk song while brushing the black paint on and knocked over the can and made a huge mess.

Being inquisitive (from growing up in a village where you knew everyone's first, middle and last name, and what book they kept on their nightstand), Jess had casually asked the neighbours about their landlord. But they didn't seem to know anything, really, except that he owned the entire property—the three flats they rented and the warehouse underneath, which he rented to JT's Roofing—and he lived somewhere in the city. A condo, Ms. Kearny believed. This left Jess free to make her own imaginative appraisal: he was single, Serbian, a drunkard, and had a Russian mafia-type personality, and her intuition told her he was one of those men with a hair-trigger temper, capable of extreme violence, maybe even gratuitous. And of course he was a rent Nazi.

Jess's mind refused to spark. She stared at the paper. She'd been there for thirty minutes without drawing a single line, not even a scrawl. Surrendering to the nothing, she placed the crayon down on the small table beside the easel, wiped her fingers on her paint-stained Levis, and then lifted the glass of red wine to her lips and inhaled before drinking the last mouthful. If her mind wandered, let it be to something other than her blunder into History or Milan—the borderline slumlord—and the seven-hundred dollars he'd bang on her door for tomorrow. She rolled her neck a few times. What she sought seemed farther away the more she thought of it, as if she was half-heartedly chasing something that didn't belong to her anymore and didn't want to be found, and it seemed that *thing* was more unattainable the longer she lived in the city. She finished the wine and placed the glass beside the crayons and got off the barstool.

Hermes sat on the waist-high bamboo Ikea stand by the window, sharing the platform with the cactus. She had thought of moving it because he liked that spot so much, but he didn't seem to mind so she'd left it. He meowed and licked his paw. She walked over and picked him up. He rubbed his head against her neck and purred, like he always did. She did her part, rocking him and scratching around his ears, and making smooching noises. She petted his back as he nestled his head over her shoulder, their comfort spot, as if she was a mother holding her baby. She was in a way.

Through the window, Jess made out a person holding an open black umbrella over their shoulder, in the parking lot of City Wide Paint across the street. Black knee-high boots, tight blue jeans. A woman. Jess watched a minute. The woman stood facing the city, the umbrella's black shade hiding her face. Then headlights cut through the light fog and a newer pick-up truck, silver like her Beetle, pulled into the parking lot and stopped in front of the woman, blocking her from Jess's view. Exhaust billowed, a moment passed, and then the truck's interior light came on and shut off. When the truck drove south toward the city, the umbrella woman was gone.

Her head ached. The bitter residue of red wine was gummy in her mouth. A grey morning pushed through the window. On the radio, which she didn't recall turning on, people were talking. She stretched out like a feline. They were arguing over the humanitarian costs of an intervention in Syria's Civil War. She sighed loudly and lifted the pillow and wrapped it around her face and ears.

There were three loud knocks on the door. She rose up from the futon. She regretted that she hadn't removed the blank paper on the easel last night. Her hair was wild, so she searched and found her hair-tie under the pillow and raked her hair back into a ponytail.

As she passed the stereo, she shut the radio off. She padded over the cold parquet floor barefoot and down the hallway to the flat's door, and when she spied through the peephole, Milan's distorted face was there. He seemed to look directly at her. In the first few months after she moved in, he'd shown up for the rent in the evening, then he started to show up in the afternoon. *Now* it was the morning. Next it would be a minute after midnight. She tucked a lock of hair behind her ear and unlocked the deadbolt. The smell of vodka wafted in on the cool air. Milan's grey ropy hair was uncombed and his eyes were bloodshot, dark rings around them like a raccoon's.

He stood there silently in his cheap tracksuit as if waiting to be invited in.

"Hello, Milan, it seems early for a visit," she said in her politely annoyed voice, mastered during dorm living at Ryerson.

He was taken aback and made sure she noticed. "Eleven o'clock isn't early. Businesses are open, people are at work."

"Not everyone works regular hours." Like her.

"Not everyone works regular jobs," he said, scratching his goatee.

Goosebumps were forming on her legs and she regretted not putting on sweatpants. "The mice are still coming in through the vents," she said, regretting also answering the door out of her weakness for responsibility. "Mice are crapping in the storage. The hallway. Even in my kitchen sink."

"After I put poison in the warehouse?" he said, shocked.

"Maybe they don't like the taste."

His mouth went slack, then he smiled and wagged his finger at her.

"It would be nice if you could try something else because as it gets colder more will be coming inside."

"Next week, I'll pick up more poison. Place it in the warehouse and storage under the stairs. Should kill the little bastards."

"Can't you try cages or like those tube things—the ones advertised on TV. Maybe a pet store would take some or I could let them go up north," she said. She felt Hermes brush against her leg before hearing him purr.

Milan gave her a puzzled look, then gestured at Hermes. "Don't let him into the storage. Might get into the poison."

"He's strictly a flat cat." Hermes purred loudly as if he knew they were speaking about him. Milan looked down and he and Hermes stared at each other.

"He hasn't caught any?"

She shook her head. "I don't think he likes the taste."

Milan grunted.

"I didn't expect you so early. I'm going out after breakfast. If you come back later this afternoon I'll have the rent for you then." If he picked up the rent on the first of the month instead of the twenty-eighth it would be much easier, easier still if he didn't demand cash and instead accepted cheque or direct deposit. Hermes darted off back into the flat.

Milan said, "See you tonight," and turned and headed down the hallway to the stairs.

After she showered, ate two Belgium waffles slathered in her grandmother's homemade blackberry jam, and drank two cups of black coffee, she dressed and strapped on her bike helmet and ipod and left the flat. There weren't any muffled actors' voices or advertisement jingles coming from Ms. Kearny's flat. On the main floor, she went around the staircase into the musty storage room and manoeuvred her ten-speed out from the stacks of flowerpots and bags of potting soil.

Jess rode south on Industrial Way, listening to Arcade Fire, into a light headwind carrying a miasma of melting plastic and depot garbage. The traffic was light. She passed by warehouses and factories and forklifts unloading trucks and parking lots full of vehicles and small groups of workers huddled together smoking and talking. She smelled pot. By the time she reached the four-kilometre marker—the billboards for Molson Canadian and Trojan Ribbed Condoms, the bottle depot on the opposite side—her head was clear. And when she arrived at the strip mall on the outskirts of the city, she felt surprisingly invigorated and couldn't help but smile at her first un-regrettable act of the day.

There were mostly trucks and vans in the parking lot. All sorts of blue-collar types filing in and out of the Tim Horton's, Subway, and CIBC. She rode up on the curb and got off her bike and placed it in the empty bike rack in front of the bank.

Inside, the queues were short, and she only had to wait a minute. The teller, Samantha, was in her thirties, perfect white teeth that reminded Jess of her porcelain toilet. Jess ran her tongue over her teeth, feeling wine residue. Overcooking the artificial pleasantries, Samantha counted out seven one-hundred dollar bills and handed them to Jess.

As she left the bank, Jess wondered if she could stand standing behind a counter all day dispensing money like an ATM. She wouldn't like it, but at least she'd have job security and benefits and no drunks ogling her or pawing her thighs and arms.

She spotted Milan's van on the other side of the parking lot as she removed her ten-speed from the rack. He sat in the driver's seat, and in the passenger seat, sat a woman wearing a purple beret and large dark sunglasses. They were just staring out the windshield. Jess thought about heading over to give him the rent now, save her a disturbance later, but she decided not to interrupt them. Maybe it was his lover and they were having a spat. She'd been there before.

On the ride home, heavy traffic sped along Industrial Way in both directions. A few times vehicles whooshed past so closely she could've reached out and touched them. With it being twelve-thirty, it was the lunch-hour rush. They worked regular jobs. After the wind from an eighteen-wheeler almost sent her careening off her ten-speed, she slowed down and stayed as close to the ditch as possible. And ten minutes later she turned right into her driveway. Mr. Holt's green Ford pick-up was parked beside her Beetle in the part of the driveway that stretched alongside the warehouse, reserved for the flat's tenants. The truck's hood was up, and Mr. Holt was leaning over the passenger fender.

They'd only spoken a few times. And this was the first time she'd seen him in a month. She thought maybe he'd been away visiting family or something, dead even crossed her mind one night after she'd drunk a few bottles of red. She rode up to the front of the truck and stopped. She heard a ratchet being worked, then a loud clunk.

"Why, why, why," he said, rising up. He thumped the engine with his palm and dropped the ratchet onto the small open toolkit. He looked at Jess and smiled as if embarrassed he'd been caught in a bout of frustration, and she thought of the blank paper upstairs on the easel. He wiped the back of his hand across his wrinkly cheek, leaving a smear of grease. Beside the toolkit, there were small engine parts and a large red book, open to a page with an engine diagram and a column of text and grease stained fingerprints.

"Sometimes I think I'm foolish tinkering with this brute. Should just drop it off at the shop down the road," he said. He removed the head from the ratchet and ran his finger over the heads in the toolkit as if he was reading Braille until he took one out and snapped it on. "My pension doesn't allow for spending sprees, barely enough to buy cigarettes. Not everyone gets a roof over their head for *free*." He nodded up at Ms. Kearney's window. The red rose bush in the window was in stark contrast to the faded-brown steel cladding on the upper-half of the building. Jess had found the bush, wilted and parched, on an upside down Smirnoff Vodka box, in her flat when she first moved in. She gave it to Ms. Kearney a few days after because it reminded Jess too much of her trip to Victoria the summer before, the night she'd been swept away and pulled farther and farther away from safety by the nostalgia of her youth and by the burden of her maturity. The night she'd given herself as freely as the busker had given her the single red rose. (A regret she wanted to forget.) Ms. Kearny reciprocated a day later when she knocked on Jess's door and gave her a rich crimson-red cushion chrysanthemum 'Bingo.' Jess managed to kill it in thirty-five days. So she bought the cactus.

"Can I help?" asked Jess, removing her helmet.

"What, join in my madness?"

"Maybe not then."

He smiled, and lifted a rag and wiped his hands off. They were shaking. "Automobiles used to be simple to work on. People think technology is a magnificent thing. Makes the one percent richer, makes harder work for us ninety-nine."

She placed her bike against the warehouse and put her helmet on the seat.

He leaned forward, shoving his hands into some dark recess. "Shine that light here."

She unhooked the light from the hood and got in closer, smelling grease and steel and cigarette smoke. He began working the ratchet.

"Ever notice people in front of the paint shop late at night?" she asked.

"No, but I never pay attention."

"Last night I saw someone, a woman. Around eleven."

"Homeless?"

"I don't think so. She got into a silver truck."

He stopped working the ratchet. "We get all sorts of transients around here. Move that light over to the left," he said. She moved the light. He started ratcheting and then came out with a bolt and dropped it with the others in the toolkit.

"How many more do you have?" she asked.

"I forgot how many questions young people ask. Five."

"Luckily I'm not busy."

He chuckled and reached the ratchet back into the engine. She positioned the light above the area, remembering the times she'd helped her grandfather work on his truck before he'd had his stroke. Mr. Holt had to be in his seventies and never had visitors. He stayed to himself, like some forgotten History tome tucked away on a library shelf collecting dust. As she held the light, she wondered where he'd been and what he'd done in his life. She wondered why he was here all alone. She'd asked herself those questions before about Ms. Kearny, too. Bubbly sixty-four-year-olds didn't fit the environment. They were both solitary people. Perhaps they were both wondering the same thing about Jess, but then she had company often: Rick, Melinda, Eve. Yes, Jess was the demographic oddity of 555A Industrial Way.

Throughout the afternoon, while listening to Satellite radio, Jess attempted to tidy up only to find herself drawn to the corner bookcase where her sketchbooks were heaped. Flipping through one, she looked at portraits of her older sister Kylie, her mother, her grandparents, other family and friends, a caricature of her boyfriend Rick. In another, there were sketches of architecture—the Brandenburg Gate, Stonehenge, the World Trade Center's Twin Towers aflame in the midst of collapsing— and in one book she'd had since fourteen, crude sketches of animals, trees, and rocks she thought resembled human faces. All the while Hermes sat beside the cactus on the Ikea stand, staring out the window, occasionally glancing at her.

Almost two hours passed before she got up and swept and mopped the parquet and dusted the furniture and washed out the cupboards, finding mouse shit in all the lower ones. The blank paper on the easel was like an enormous vacant eye. It kept reminding her of the empty feeling inside every time she sat down to perform the simple motions she'd performed for years. She was torturing herself by reminding herself. At five o'clock she turned the easel around so the eye faced the wall. She continued to clean and it wasn't until the linen was in the dryer that she checked the time: five to six.

She and Rick had made plans for a movie night and had agreed on six-thirty. With Rick that meant more like seven, maybe seven-thirty. She lit two cinnamon candles and put on some jazz.

There were times when she welcomed the shower's strong water pressure. Tonight was one of them. It massaged her tense neck and shoulders and she thought how that tenseness had come only in the last year as the consequences of her choices bore down on her like an oppressive regime on its people. Questioning herself why she was still residing on Industrial Way had lost all novelty. Andrea was back home working at Rocky Crest. Her degree cost half as much and took half as long as Jess's. Andrea was a twenty-minute drive from work, close to family and friends, enjoying a tourism career in a field in which there would always be steady, well-paying employment, like her sister, like the bank teller, benefits and security. And Jess was here on the outskirts of the outskirts, searching empty-heartedly for a job in her miss-chosen field, serving tables at Dino's Sports Pub, rebuffing bottom-rung married businessmen and young macho hotheads with far too much testosterone and far too little grey matter. Trying to kick-start her enthusiasm and ambition, trying to figure out what her next step in life should be at a point where all her friends seemed to know, like her sister knew, like she was supposed to know. And now she couldn't even draw, crude lines or fine lines, nothing. What did everyone back home think and say about the choices she'd made? Her life as an uninspired History major, waiting tables with a future as bleak as the miles of chain-link fences and soviet-era drab buildings that hedged Industrial Way, the road she had chosen out of some naïve and foolish whisper. A whisper that had never returned to guide her. It was as if she had intentionally self-sabotaged herself for some romantic idea of independence, all that she'd thought about since Kylie had moved to Naples six years ago to teach English and travel around Europe and the Far East, like some adventurous debutante in a fling with life. Their mother had had the same ideas, Jess's grandmother had warned first Kylie and later Jess (*not practical, down right foolish*), before she'd embarked on a pilgrimage to Mount Baldy in California to seek enlightenment from Buddha, only to find Los Angeles, addiction, and death. Jess had revisited her mother's calamitous downward spiral so many times that she was as numb to it as she imagined her mother was—stoned on tranquilizers and booze—when she swerved across three lanes and collided with an off-ramp meridian. And now it was Jess's turn, only she was about to collide with reality. Maybe she had already and was clueless to the fact. Life stared at her now like that vacant eye had been staring at her for weeks—void, with no intention of collaborating. The water from the shower nozzle was cooling. She had lost track of time. And the tank had lost hot water.

Jess dried and brushed her hair. She put on a pair of holey jeans and a navy-blue turtleneck sweater she'd taken from her grandfather's closet, before her grandmother donated all of his clothes to the Salvation Army in Bracebridge. In the kitchen, she removed a bottle of Van Dirk's u-brew red wine from the pantry and poured herself a glass. Only three bottles were left, and she was sure when she counted last week there'd been eight. Perhaps the mice were carting them off back to their nests, sipping u-brew wine, getting filthy drunk and singing karaoke in the walls with bugs for back-up singers.

Hermes was sitting on the Ikea stand, his eyes fixed on her. "Are you drinking my wine?" she cooed.

He licked his nose and hopped down and scampered to the bedroom. Someone knocked on the door. She glanced at the clock on the kitchen wall: seven p.m. Glass in hand, she walked down the hallway and put her eye to the peephole. She expected to see Rick with one eye closed, fish-hooking one side of his cheek, tongue hanging out, inches away because he knew she always checked the peephole. Instead Milan's red veiny nose greeted her like 3D. She yelled for him to hang on a second and rushed to the bedroom and picked up the envelope of rent money off the maple dresser. As she started to leave, she realized the glass of wine was still in her hand. She took a quick drink and set the glass down on the dresser beside a photo of Kylie and her boyfriend, Bonito, holding hands in front of the Blue Mosque in Istanbul.

When she opened the door, she couldn't smell vodka or cigar. Gum, Juicy Fruit.

"I'm late, sorry," said Milan. His voice was less arrogant, his hair combed. He wasn't in the same state as he'd been that morning.

"Any luck with the cages or mice tubes?" she asked.

He shook his head.

She handed him the envelope which he slid into the pocket of his black leather jacket. He wore dark blue jeans, black loafers. Not exactly snazzy but better than his usual attire of soccer tracksuits. They stared awkwardly as if both waiting for the other to speak. Then Milan said, "I'll return later this week, put down more traps and poison." He turned and headed down the hall.

Jess heard the steel door open at the bottom of the stairwell, and then close, then footsteps up the stairs. Rick and Milan nodded as they passed each other. Rick grinned and winked at Jess. He carried a six-pack of Corona and a Ben's Video bag.

"Your landlord's dressed like a gigolo," he whispered as he entered.

She punched him playfully on the shoulder and shut the door. "He's probably got a date or something. Look who's talking—long-john shirt, Carharts, workboots."

"It's my style."

"What? Not-changed-or-showered style."

They walked into the living room. Hermes popped his head out of the bathroom door and scampered up to Rick and brushed against his leg a few times. Rick knelt down and scratched around his ears, then Hermes shot down the hall and vanished into the bathroom.

"I saw a woman in the paint shop parking lot the other night, at eleven o'clock."

"Doing what?"

"She just stood there holding an umbrella. A truck picked her up."

"Could've been a hooker. Less chance of being busted, I guess, if they're away from downtown. Is Don Juan gonna take care of the mice?" Rick went into the kitchen.

"I asked for cages to trap them. He said poison."

"He needs an exterminator."

"It's not that bad."

"No, but then you'd have to stay at my place for a week." He put a Corona on the counter and placed the others in the fridge.

"What about Hermes?"

"I'm sure he could find a place to bed down. A workboot maybe, or old blanket or something." He popped the cap off the bottle with the opener he'd fastened to the side of the cupboard months ago.

"I don't think he'd settle for anything besides the foot of my bed, on my duvet."

Hermes was back in the living room, standing motionless and watching them both.

"He was feral seven months ago. And had fleas."

"He wasn't feral. He was starving and looking for a home. And he had a collar. Probably abandoned by some jerk."

"Get out of this place. Move downtown closer to me."

"What movies did you get?" she asked.

"Rick lifted the bag off the counter. "I went with Kubrick. *Full Metal Jacket* and *Eyes Wide Shut* were all they had at Ben's. *Clockwork Orange* is missing." Rick suggested they start with *Eyes Wide Shut*. She said she'd like to start with the earlier of the two and see how Kubrick developed as a director. Rick said he couldn't argue with her rational.

As *Eyes Wide Shut* ended, Rick brushed his fingertips on her neck and she felt a tingle down her spine, her nipples hardened. She stretched her arms back and he slid her shirt over her head. They had sex while the credits played.

They were still lying on the futon when she woke. The menu screen for *Eyes Wide Shut* was on the TV. Cozy and tired. She felt Rick's heartbeat against her back. She wanted another glass of wine, but she didn't want to un-nestle herself from the warmth and comfort of his body, go into the kitchen and open the cupboard, and see only the few bottles left, take one and feel guilty. She almost shut her eyes when she saw Hermes sitting on the Ikea stand, not unusual except that his nose was pressed against the window. A circle of condensation had formed, rivulets running down, as if he'd been there for quite awhile. He was an Egyptian statue beside the cactus.

Jess slowly lifted Rick's arm off her shoulder and got up naked and padded over to the window. She scratched around Hermes' ears. He didn't purr or even flinch. Outside the asphalt glistened, and in the paint-shop's parking lot stood umbrella woman, the black shade hiding her face. Jess felt exposed in the window, so she moved to the side and peeked around the jamb. The woman strolled back and forth along the sidewalk, twirling her umbrella, raising and lowering her hand in which she held a smoke.

A few minutes passed, then headlights. A black luxury sedan appeared, a Cadillac Jess thought. It slowed down and drove into the parking lot and stopped in front of umbrella woman. The woman leaned inside the driver's window. She swayed her hips side-to-side, then she rose up and shut the umbrella and shook off the rain. She had short red hair plastered to her head, a black scarf around her neck. She glanced up at Jess's window before she sauntered around to the passenger door of the sedan and slipped inside. The driver headed south. Hermes hadn't moved, and when Jess lifted him up his body was like a piece of driftwood. She stroked him for a minute and he relaxed in her arms and nestled against her chest, his head draped over her shoulder.

"Who is she? What's this all about?" She rubbed her cheek against his hair.

He began to purr. His body relaxed even more.

"I'm thinking the same thing," she said. She drew a heart with her finger in the condensation. She passed Rick on the futon and carried Hermes to the bedroom.

When she arrived at home, she noticed Ms. Kearney had removed the red rose bush from the window. Jess opened the trunk of the Beetle and reached inside and lifted out two hemp grocery bags. There was an oil stain where Mr. Holt's truck had been parked. She shut the trunk and carried the two bags up the driveway and unlocked the steel door and entered the stairwell. As she took the stairs, Ms. Kearny appeared from the storage room, cradling a stack of small green flowerpots to her chest.

She had fresh curls in her hair and wore a gardening apron, dark brown gloves. Last time Jess had stopped for a brief chat with Ms.

Kearny, the chat had stretched into three hours of Earl Grey tea and bits of gossip snatched from the British tabloids that Ms. Kearny kept heaped on her kitchen table, some dating back to the 90s. Classics, Ms. Kearny called them, worth a fortune to a collector one day.

"I do this every week now or so it seems," said Ms. Kearney. She lifted the flower pots. Jess continued up the stairs, Ms. Kearny behind her. "Saw you help Stewart with his truck the other day. He can be a grump. No one in his life. You know Milan gave him that truck, just up and gave it to him one day. Lucky, too, 'cause the old Buick he owned was about to fall apart. He doesn't know that I know but I do. I know Milan got him a job cleaning offices, too. A few nights a week."

"You took the rose down," said Jess.

"Didn't feel it should be up there right now, that's all."

"Why don't you store some of those flower pots in your flat."

"But, dear, this is my exercise. I'd blow up like Oprah if I didn't have these stairs," she said, her voice hushed.

"Heaven forbid, Ms. Kearny."

Jess knew she didn't leave her flat all that much. Jess had seen her a block south a few times at the bottle depot, but Ms. Kearny seemed content with her life here on Industrial Way, hooked on paparazzi induced headlines and drama from across the pond. Jess wondered how often she was alone. She had no children, never spoke about family, except for her dead husband once while Jess was visiting. Her chin had started to quiver and she hurried into the kitchen and poured hot water from a kettle that hadn't yet whistled, to steep their third pot of tea. She returned, carrying a plate of rum balls and talking about Princess Di conspiracies.

Jess was sure Ms. Kearny was lonely and she thought of her grandmother in Bala, who always had family or friends visiting, sometimes both: her life entwined with the community—bridge and town meetings and bingo and crafts.

Jess took the last step. Ms. Kearny was right behind her, huffing away. When Jess reached the flat door, she paused. Ms. Kearny was about to enter her flat.

"Ms. Kearny, there's been a woman out front of the paint shop at night. Twice now."

Ms. Kearny's fingers rested on her doorknob. "Must've been a vagrant. They come and go around here once and awhile," she said, without turning to face Jess. "Two summers ago they stole a bag of soil I'd left outside. Couldn't figure out why they'd do that."

The homeless at the south end of Industrial Way wore mismatched clothing, shuffling around, picking through garbage bins. Some pushed shopping carts, wheeling about their meagre possessions. "No, I don't think so. She carried an umbrella, and two different vehicles picked her up."

"Don't know, dear." She opened her door and said, "Doubt you'll see her again," and hurried inside and shut the door.

Jess stood holding the groceries, focused on the spot where Ms. Kearny had been a moment ago before fleeing an opportunity to chat.

*

Over the next three days, Jess left for work at noon and returned home by nine-thirty p.m. She had an urge to turn the vacant eye around on the second night and make an attempt to draw. Instead she uncorked a bottle of red. She watched the talking heads on CBC and CNN discuss the millions of Syrian refugees, debate on the right course of action, as if the West was a puppet master ready to tug and swing a marionette, make it jig and dance.

The last two bottles were gone by Wednesday, so come Thursday on her way home from work she stopped at the LCBO. And for the first time in six months, she bought and drank wine that she hadn't made. She thought about stopping at Van Dirk's u-brew winery, but then Mr. Van Dirk would be forced to present her with an award for Most Brewed Batches in a Year by an Under 30. And she wasn't big on awards.

When she arrived home, she checked her cellphone for messages. Rick had called from Niagara Falls, where his brother's company was renovating a casino. As usual, he rambled on for over a minute, which she always bugged him about but really always thought how very cute it was. He explained some of the history of the falls, which he'd picked up from a travel brochure, and then he told her how awe-inspiring they were (like her) and how he'd like to spend a weekend there together.

Come eleven o'clock, Jess was watching an 80s documentary on KCTS about South American Juntas. Reagan—the actor—beat the rhetoric drum, warning of the dangers of a communist expansion in the Americas and domino effects and total nuclear war. Hermes slid off the futon and sneaked over the floor and leapt onto the Ikea stand. He fixed on something outside.

Jess smooched and waited for him to return. He didn't move, so she shut off the TV and went over to the window. Umbrella woman was there only this time she carried no umbrella. She faced north. She puffed on a smoke, the cherry flashing orange. When she finished it, she lit another. Jess and Hermes watched. She paced back and forth, glancing at the warehouse. A small car slowed down while driving past, then made a U-turn and pulled into the paint shop and stopped in front of her. It had a dent in the driver's front fender. Jess wasn't sure of the make or model, but thought it was dark green. This time umbrella woman didn't lean in the window and talk, she simply opened the passenger door, and as she slipped in, she flicked her smoke onto the asphalt. The car sat idle a minute, then drove north.

Jess lifted Hermes by the belly and hugged him and padded over to the easel. She turned it around and faced the vacant eye. She sat down on the stool with Hermes on her lap and lifted a crayon and began to sketch.

When Jess arrived home from the LCBO and Van Dirk's (without the award), Milan's dark blue mini-van was behind Mr. Holt's Ford. She parked beside the van, leaving enough room for Mr. Holt to back out if he needed to leave. She gathered up her purse and cellphone and the wine and stepped out into a light rain that had been falling all morning.

Milan appeared from around the front of the van, a black FIFA cap tugged low, carrying an empty box. Smirnoff Vodka. "I put down more traps and poison in the warehouse." His eyes were bloodshot, his schnozz red with veins like spiderwebs. She caught a whiff of cigar and vodka. Maybe he'd been on a bender.

"No cages or tubes?"

"No, lots of poison." He glanced down at the LCBO bag that held two bottles of Okanogan Zinfandel. Her face warmed and she regretted not using one of her canvas bags. It was Milan, though, and he probably had a bottle of vodka on the seat of his van and a stocked bar at home. His eyes narrowed and he flicked a conspiratorial grin. "I need to make a stop, too," he said, gesturing the box toward the bag.

Jess lifted it up, the bottles clunking together.

"Yeah, there's a deal on Canadian wine—two for the price of one," she said nonchalantly.

He opened the van's sliding door. The back seat was missing. "Haven't drunk wine in ten years," he said.

Jess would've been fifteen and tasted wine only a few times at holidays when an aunt or uncle had asked if she wanted a sip. Ten years was a long time. In the last six months, she hadn't gone ten days without a few glasses. He leaned in and placed the box down amidst a pell-mell of newspapers and another box that looked to be stuffed with clothing. There was a large blue cooler behind the passenger seat, a bungee cord holding the lid on. He slid the door shut and turned to her. "My wife Zebrine and I used to listen to Flamenco music and drink French wine or plum brandy."

She'd never seen him wearing a wedding band. "I didn't know you were married," she said.

"Not anymore. She died years ago."

"I'm sorry. My mother died when I was eight and—"

"I have a thick hide," he said, swatting his forearm. He brushed a grey flock of hair from his forehead. He reached inside his jacket pocket and removed a pack of Export A Regular and a Zippo with two eagle heads on it. He put a smoke in his mouth, offered her one. She waved him off.

"I think there's been a prostitute hanging around the paint shop at night."

He turned to the paint shop, his face deadpan, and lifted the Zippo with a slightly trembling hand and lit the smoke, leaving her statement hanging in the air.

"She just walks back and forth smoking. I saw her on three different nights. She left in three different vehicles." It began to rain harder.

Milan tilted his head back at the lead sky. He dragged lazily on the smoke dangling from his lips, and exhaled. "Street people wander by here all the time."

"Neighbours said the same thing."

He shrugged his shoulders. "People come and go for different reasons. It's the fringes of the city. Kids race sports cars. Thieves burned a car one time. Remember the hoodlum graffiti? If she returns let me know. My friend is a cop. He can drive by at night."

"Do you think she's a prostitute?"

"Call me if she comes back." He opened the door and climbed in the van.

Jess washed her bed linen and then scrubbed the sink, bathtub, toilet. Either Rick had missed the toilet last weekend or Hermes had attempted to use it and failed. She doubted the latter. At eight o'clock, her cellphone rang emitting the hammer ring-tone. It was Rick. He said they were driving north on the Trans-Canada, but they wouldn't be back until later than expected so could he wear her semi-manly grey sweatpants and the Toronto Maple Leafs jersey that he'd bought her last Christmas. She said as long as he behaved himself, and from now on when he woke up to use the toilet, he take better aim. He denied her claim. She said he should try sitting down to go. He refused out of duty to manhood, then asked her if she could pick up the Sandler flicks because he wouldn't be back in time and didn't want her to download them since Ben's Video was on the cusp of shutting its doors permanently, and he'd been renting from there since he was a kid. She agreed while pouring her first glass of zinfandel. He asked her if her hookah was operational. She said it could be if she wanted it to, but then added they'd smoked all the Turkish-mint tobacco a month ago. He said he remembered. She giggled and he laughed and said he'd see her in a few hours.

From the bedroom closet, she removed her blue and white Helle Hanson jacket and slipped it on, and a minute later left the flat. Jess could hear TV voices coming from Ms. Kearney's as she took the stairs. When she opened the door, something brushed in-between her calves. She knew it was Hermes before she saw him bolt down the driveway, his tail straight up, his white backside disappearing behind Mr. Holt's Ford.

Jess stood in the doorway. Dumbfounded. He'd never left the flat since she'd found him scrounging around the warehouse eight months ago. He never expressed any desire to leave. The only curiosity he'd shown for the outside world was what he could see outside the window. The rain was really coming down, so Jess lifted her hood and went out after him, calling his name. After searching around the Ford and Beetle, satisfied he wasn't hiding underneath either, she headed out to the front of the warehouse. She would've been drenched if she hadn't put on her Helle Hanson, just as Hermes would be drenched unless he'd found shelter. One of JT's roofing trucks was parked in front of the warehouse, ladders on the roof racks. She bent over and scanned underneath, calling him, smelling oil from the asphalt. Nothing. She made the smooching sound. Still nothing.

She rounded the far corner of the warehouse into the narrow concrete alley. The cinderblock wall of the welding shop next door rose high. There were no spare tires or ladders or garbage cans or anything else she'd pictured there. Maybe Hermes was confused. He hadn't been outside forever, could've lost his outdoor skills. She walked out to the road, hearing a fence rattling in the wind. A taxi swooshed past going south, followed by a truck. They didn't slow down. They didn't give a flying fuck about a person on the side of the road, in a downpour, frantically searching for something, obviously distressed, definitely looking out of place. If she was in Bala, everyone would've stopped. She hated this city, and the assholes populating it.

She searched around the vehicles again. She huffed and threw her arms out and cursed under her breath. He must've found some shelter, she decided. She stormed to the door and flung it open and went inside. As she climbed the stairs, she thought of the trips to the vet, of the canned tuna and salmon, of the scratching post—albeit used yet high quality. Then she thought of all the times she'd allowed him the comfort of her bed and duvet, and of her boobs—admittedly there wasn't a whole lot there but he never seemed to mind. She'd lifted him from the gutter and given him a home. Hell, she'd even taken him to Bala four times to visit family and friends. More than Rick.

By the time Rick arrived a few hours later, Jess had been out twice searching, and both times had found nothing. Rick came in with a smile, cheery, oblivious to the fact that she was two hours into a situation, and when his mouth slowly opened, his eyes widened, she thought how foolish the whole thing was. Shitty but foolish. He dropped his bag on the parquet and followed her inside, the draft from the hall carrying the smell of wood-glue and sawdust.

"I didn't pick up the movies—Hermes took off. I've been searching for him for hours," she said. "It's been pouring non-stop and I'm sure he's out there hiding until the rain lets up."

"Ah, that's why the cinderblock's propping the door open." He ran a hand through his wet hair and nodded back toward the door. "You want me to go out and find him."

She shook her head. "No, no, he's fine, probably found shelter."

"Why don't I take the catnip out there, lure him back?"

"Did you leave the brick in the door."

"I took it out, but I'll put it back."

"I'll make coffee."

Over the next twenty minutes, Rick filled her in on the casino they were renovating. He was animated, passionate, like always when he talked carpentry. She guessed he was trying to take her mind off Hermes because he was talking faster than usual. And then she guessed he was able to tell that she wasn't really into it because he stopped mid-explanation, while telling her about purple-heart crown moulding. He suggested they go for a drive, nothing serious, and see if they could spot Hermes. It wasn't raining anymore, he added, so Hermes might be out and about, ready to be rescued or sowing wild oats or doing whatever else feral cats do after a spell with domestication. She said no, that he'd be fine, but she heard uncertainty in her voice. So did Rick. He said he'd drive as he scooped her keys off the kitchen counter.

They drove north first, away from the city. The sky was a mix of bright stars and smoky clouds. The wind had already dried large patches of asphalt. As Rick putted along, she scanned the front of the warehouses and factories and commercial businesses. Whenever she saw a flicker of black or a waver in the shadows, she asked him to slow down.

A truck raced up behind them, headlights burst into the Beetle. Rick flicked the blinker on and the truck sped by and Jess pictured Hermes bolting onto the road in front of the truck, like the raccoon did that she'd hit on Highway 69 last summer on the way to Parry Sound. She hadn't stopped and she *loved* animals. She doubted the driver of truck would.

At the end of the Industrial Way, they came to the head of a T. Rural homes and farms stretched for miles, lights dotting the landscape, fences parcelling the land. The road was empty. Rick turned the Beetle around and headed south. Everything began to blur in a mass of industry by the time they reached the warehouse. Rick said he'd go in and check to see if Hermes was there. He pulled into the driveway and parked and got out and went inside. Jess placed her elbow on the door, rested her head in her palm. The wind was stronger now, moving the clouds, buffeting the Beetle, whistling through the man-made tangle. Then Rick appeared in the headlights shaking his head.

As they putted south, they passed a long string of on-coming vehicles. Workers heading home after a shift. And again she pictured Hermes getting run down. They didn't talk. The lights on the Trojan Condoms billboard were flashing as if shorting out.

Rick turned into the bottle depot and stopped the car. "Let's pick up coffee. Do some more passes," he said with conviction, as if he was ready to road warrior all night if need be.

She rubbed her left temple, feeling defeated and wiped. "No, no, just go back. We could be out here all night putzing around and still not find him."

"Hey, what if I drive slower. Crank up Tragically Hip or 54-40, lure him out. I can see it. Hermes running alongside the car," he said, running his fingers over the dash. "His ears blowing in the wind, leap right in the window—voila—land on your lap, curl up against your neck."

They both started laughing, from deep down, the kind you rarely felt but when you did you wished you laughed like it all the time and wished for it to go on and on. Her eyes started to water. By the time they stopped, the windows were foggy and she felt dizzy. She bowed her head and massaged the bridge of her nose, then wound the window down, letting in cool air. Milan's van was under an overhang at one of the depot's loading docks. He stood outside the van, his black cap pulled low, beside a woman wearing a dark hat with earflaps and black puffy jacket stitched with grey duct tape. There was a shopping cart with a blue tote and a few green garbage bags inside.

Jess was about to point it out to Rick.

"Is that your landlord propositioning a bum?" he asked.

She didn't answer as Milan opened the van's sliding door and leaned inside. He came out with articles of clothing and handed them to the woman. She placed them in the blue tote. They exchanged a few words and then she trundled toward the city.

"Yeah, that's him," she said quietly.

"He doesn't seem like the charitable type."

"What's that mean?" She turned to Rick.

He raised his hands, palms toward her. "You told him at least a dozen times about the mice before he got on with the poison and traps."

"And where was my knight-in-shining armour? Didn't see you rush over with cages or tubes."

"Tubes? You said he was a borderline slumlord. That's all. And remember—a violent streak."

A figure emerged from behind the bottle depot, a man with a dark mop of hair and scraggly beard. On his back was a large red backpack, sleeping bag tied to the bottom.

"Jesuschrist, he's running a drive-thru thrift store," said Rick.

The interior of the car had cooled so Jess wound up the window. Rick turned on the heat and hot air whooshed from the dash vent.

Milan gave the man a brown paper lunch bag. They shook hands, spoke to each other. Then the man readjusted the backpack and put his head down and walked back along the side of the depot.

"Let's go, maybe Hermes is at home," said Jess.

The warehouse door was still ajar, but Hermes wasn't inside the stairwell or upstairs in front of the flat. Inside Jess took off her shoes and put on her pink furry slippers and went into the living room and flicked on the standing lamp in the corner. Her defeated feeling was replaced by a begrudging acceptance: Hermes wouldn't return tonight, maybe he'd never return. But why had he waited until tonight to take off? Why not yesterday or last week or last month? Why in the rain? He hated baths. She'd only seen one other cat lurking around, wild and scrawny, and that was months ago so it wasn't like he was out chumming with the robust feline community. Rick said he was going to take a shower.

When he turned the shower on, she poured herself a glass of zinfandel, and then went into the living room. She paused in front of the window and looked out. She spotted Hermes immediately. He was sitting in the paint shop parking lot and seemed to be staring up at her. Jess put her glass down on the Ikea stand, pricking the back of her hand on the cactus, and rushed out of the flat with only her pink furries on her feet.

By the time she reached the end of the warehouse's driveway, he was gone. She started across the road and caught a flash of white from his backside. Hermes ran in-between the far wall of the paint shop and the large blue shipping container beside it. She ran and tripped out of one slipper, so she kicked the other off and picked them both up. She couldn't see anything in the narrow corridor formed by the cinder-block wall and container. She turned sideways and entered. Her days of walking barefoot on Lake Joe's pebbly shores were long past.

The soles of her feet absorbed the cold and she shivered. The smell of damp brick and rust was heavy as she inched along in the darkness and smooched for Hermes. It was like the paddy wagon they had all been rounded up in during the G20 protests. The container was on a slight angle and bottlenecked the farther along she moved. She had to shimmy like an urban spelunker, her back against the brick wall. What if she got wedged? Like those Santa burglars in the chimneys. Rick didn't know where she was. She only had on jeans and a sweater. What about hypothermia? What if she froze to death?

When she popped out on the other side, her eyes slowly adjusted to the darkness of the closed-in area. She called Hermes. Her voice sounded unnatural and angry. So she smooched but even that sound was perverted. She dropped her slippers and put them back on. There were no openings in the chain-link fence at the end of the building. She rounded the container and walked along the far side.

He didn't want to be found. Simple. That was it. What had she done to cause this? What had she done so that he now refused her home— and her? Maybe he didn't like the domestic life. He didn't like mice so maybe he wanted to hunt birds or squirrels. Shit like that. Rejoin the urban-wildlife food chain.

As Jess neared the front of the container, about to step out from its shadow, she spotted umbrella woman. She carried a closed umbrella in one hand and a lit smoke in the other. She'd changed her red hair to black, her brown leather jacket and blue jeans were tight, accentuating her tall thin body.

Did she cough? Did she say hello and strike up a conversation? Or did she just cross to the warehouse like an apparition that didn't want to spook anyone, that hoped not to be seen. Before she could make up her mind, there were headlights. From the direction of the city. Jess slinked back into the shadow just as a van appeared and wheeled into the paint shop, the headlights exposing Jess momentarily. If the driver noticed, they didn't show it. Then Jess recognized the van. It was Milan's.

He stopped directly in front of the woman and slammed the van into park and opened the door, the interior light turning on. He got out and rushed around the hood and strode up to umbrella woman until they were face-to-face.

"What is this?" said Milan, gesturing his hand back to the warehouse. "What are you doing? Pestering the tenants. Embarrassing yourself. You frightened the new girl."

She didn't flinch, and said, "You mean embarrass you, Milan Tannic. The mighty soldier who packed up his family and ran away from his homeland."

"So this is why, to shame me?" he asked. He lowered his voice. "What we went through, Elsa. You don't know. Decisions we had to make. We came to Canada so you could have a better life."

"All my life the same cliché. What was here for me, Milan Tannic?"

"Don't call me that, call me father. I'm your father, Elsa."

"My father," she said, her voice high. "He's been dead since *she* died. Before even."

Milan shook his head as if he didn't want to hear anymore. "Where does this come from, why do you do this to yourself, to me, to your mother's memory." He outstretched his arms and fingers and flung them up and down. "Stop the drugs. Stop all of this."

"Give me one reason why I should. One reason you fucking hypocrite. You can't even talk or walk you're so drunk on vodka. I can see it on you like plague on a rat." She turned toward Jess, crossing her arms, then back to Milan. "You gambled and drank and womanized. You and your fellow ex-pats. While she was dying. You make me sick. Still. Two years later."

"So in spite you sell everything I gave you and run off. Leave the place a mess—to be a hussy?

She swung the umbrella at his hand and missed. "I'm not a junker you can fix-up by slapping on new tires and a muffler. Not one of your tenants or vagrants you can give things to, make yourself feel better for a lifetime of sins. You can't fix what you've broken in here," she said, pounding her chest. She took a few strides toward Jess and stopped.

All of it made sense to Jess. And she felt awkward then, learning about their private history, hearing it painfully revealed in a way that wasn't meant for anyone else to hear. She felt small, petty. She had an urge to abandon the shadows, allow guilt to wash over her as she ran across the road, up the driveway, and up the stairs to the flat.

Elsa stood facing the paint shop, Milan a few feet behind her. He reached out again and went to place his hand on her shoulder. She shrugged away before it landed and stepped forward into the light of the paint shop. She was striking, haunting, her black hair was sculpted and glistened and looked like a nest of baby garter snakes. Her large dark eyes—unmistakably her father's—were drowsy, wrapped in smoky circles, and her lean bony face and full lips gave her the look of a fading European model who'd done far too much drugs.

"We can get you help. Treatment."

She swiped the back of her silver-ringed hand over one eye, then the other. She sniffled.

"Let me help you," he said. "I know a place. I spoke to them before you left. They said they could help. We can—"

"Since when did it become we? *Since when?*"

He yanked off his hat and smacked it against his thigh and clenched the brim in both hands and twisted as if wringing out a dishtowel. "Please, Elsa."

"Not a fucking chance. They pin you down and snow you with tranquilizers in those places. Might as well be in prison. In Texas or Iraq."

Milan reached both arms out tentatively but stopped and lowered them. They stood quiet and silent a moment. Then he put his hat back on and straightened his back, cleared his throat, and pointed at the van. "Come to the bank. I'll give you money so you don't need to do what you're doing, for at least awhile. You can stop these ... these transactions for love."

Hermes appeared suddenly from the other side of the container and whisked over the asphalt toward the van. Elsa's eyes grew. She smiled and opened her arms. Jess was about to step out and call Hermes when he leapt to Elsa's chest. She hugged him tightly and rocked him from side to side, as if they'd been performing the act of affection for years. And Jess tried to recall if it was her or Hermes who'd started it all those months ago. But couldn't.

Elsa turned, Hermes' head resting on her shoulder. Milan went to the passenger door and opened it. Elsa looked up at the flat's faintly-lit window, where Jess and Hermes had watched her from over the last week, and then she rounded the hood and climbed into the van and shut the door. Milan hurried to the other side.

Hermes opened his eyes and—Jess was sure—looked at her in the shadows.

Left or Right

Marco was leaning against the tailgate of his Escalade, casual, puffing a smoke, staring off at the glow over Winnipeg, as he waited for whoever it was to arrive so they could do the dirt. He didn't know what kind of dirt. Maybe it was picking up a few kilos of meth or cocaine, or pancaking a hand with a ball-peen hammer. Maybe it was breaking an arm or kidnapping or extorting someone for a little, or maybe a whole lot. Most of the time the boys didn't tell him shit, just gave him the order that he obeyed. Sometimes it came at noon, at ten o'clock at night, or at one in the morning like this time. He'd long ago given up caring about the nature of the dirt, because by doing dirt he was inching his way farther into the club. And he'd heard a rumour—his days as a prospect were almost finished.

When he had quiet moments like this, rare now in his life of excitement, he pictured himself on a boat like Hansel's or Cookie's, anchored out in the middle of Lake Winnipeg, drinking, wheeling broads, enjoying the power and respect and brotherhood that came along with the patch. He pictured himself cruising down the highway on his soft-tail, flying his colors, drivers pulling out of the way and other bikers keeping their distance out of fear. After three years of the boys treating him like a puppet he would soon have it all. Exactly what he'd always wanted.

Headlights cut up and down through the night as a vehicle drove toward him. They blinded Marco, making him feel exposed and vulnerable before he raised a hand, dodging out of the glare. He made out a truck, its leaf springs creaking along the washboard gravel. And he wondered who it was for the first time since he got the call from Cookie an hour ago. The truck's brakes squealed as it neared, thick exhaust billowed from the tailpipe, the smell strong in the wind. It was an older Dodge, early 80s he guessed, dark blue, the ram head on the hood glinting in the moonlight. There were truck panels on top of the box, forming almost a pen, made of horizontal wooden slats so tightly together he couldn't see through them. A blue tarp stretched over top, tied down by orange twine at random spots, rusty fenders, like a thousand other trucks driving around the province. Marco couldn't see who was driving because the windows were tinted with do-it-yourself tint, the type that always ended up looking like shit with bubbles. The driver stopped just past his truck on the other side of the gravel road, then put it into park and shut off the headlights.

Marco took a final long drag on his smoke, exhaled, and flicked the butt to the earth. He then stood there waiting for whoever was inside to get out. A minute passed, the engine pinging. Marco tugged his parka cuff up and glanced at his Rolex, making a big deal of it. He wasn't patient; his rep had been built on a full-bore attitude.

Marco began mean-mugging the truck, when the driver, as if sensing his impatience, opened the door a crack, stopped, then squeaked it open wide and stepped out. He was tall, a blue toque pulled low on a heavy brow, real primitive looking.

Marco was sure he'd never seen him before tonight. Marco crossed the road, searching for the man's eyes, but was unable to find them at the back of his sockets. And the scruff on his chops made Marco think he didn't care for a razor, or couldn't afford one. He wore dark blue mechanic's coveralls, with grease stains and a name tag on the left side of the chest in fancy letters: Eddy.

"You gotta be Marco," said Eddy in a throaty voice, extending a hand.

Marco smelled garlic coming off him. "Let's get this done so I can go home." He ignored the hand, which hung there a sec. The cold treatment.

Eddy nodded and headed around to the back of the truck. Marco followed close behind, noticing how tightly the coveralls stretched across Eddy's wide back and long arms. Marco was reminded of the orangutans he and Charla had seen at the Toronto Zoo the summer before. The club recruited all types of loons to do dirt. Hansel said these guys were like the tools they used to work on their bikes—some were screwdrivers, others ratchets or wrenches. It all depended on the job, because you needed the right tool for the right job. But use them like tools. Marco smiled foxy. What type of tool was Eddy? Vice grips? Eddy yanked on the tailgate's handle and lowered it, then stood aside, revealing a large rusty barrel strapped to a trolley under the tarp. He stepped aside, kinda bowed, and rolled and waved his hand like he was a game show host presenting a could-have prize to a could-be lucky contestant. Trying to be a funny guy. Marco caught a whiff of something funky. "What the fuck's in there?"

"Oil, moonshine, gold, maybe a barrel of laughs—got no fucking idea. Don't care to know," he said. Marco saw a flash of large white teeth that made him think of tusks. There was something different about this tool. Maybe a bit loonier than the usual.

"You're alright," said Marco and he stuck out his hand for a shake. The hot treatment. Wouldn't be long before it chilled right the fuck off again. The treatment gave him a sense of power.

"Eddy," he said. Marco's hand disappeared, engulfed in a black mechanic glove.

Eddy had a pussy handshake, definitely not vice grips: Marco settled on pliers.

When Eddy let go, he looked at Marco's hand. "Those are glitzy rings, like that truck of yours. Sure you don't want to take them off before, you know," he clicked his tongue, nodded toward the barrel, "we handle this."

Marco thought of all the money, vehicles, and electronics, all the gold and diamonds and even tools—both the real and people kind— he'd extorted, and all the bones he'd broken and all the savage dirt he'd done while wearing his rings. He warped them so regularly he'd bought a ring-sizer and jeweller's hammer to fix them, that being the only time he would take them off. This tool had no fucking idea what Marco was about. Maybe he thought Marco was a punk. "I'll be alright," he said, snappy. "Let's get this done."

"What's your rush? Enjoy nature, you never know when they'll dig for potash or drill for oil, bleed it all—"

"What are you some kinda tree fucker? I got things to do." Char was waiting at home. She wasn't known for her patience either. One of the reasons they got along so well. And he was twenty hours away—give or take—from kneeling down in front of her and asking if she wanted to be his, locking her into submission with a ring. He'd been carrying it around in his pocket for two weeks. A two karat princess-cut Canadian diamond from a mine in the Yukon. Even had a number he could type in online to watch it being mined. Un-fucking real. Char would love that. Always smart to have a woman kicking around the house full-time, to clean up and keep the bed warm and cook dinner, shit like that, as Hansel would say every time he saw a tight little ass pass by.

Eddy's mouth spread, showing his tusks again. "And let me guess, you got people to see."

This loon did think he was a funny guy and Marco pissed on funny guys, usually after he dropped them onto their backs, as they were choking on their blood and busted teeth. It felt like someone had snapped open his throttle, got his piston ramming in his chest. He huffed and climbed up onto the tailgate. Hunching under the tarp, he took a few whiffs and decided the funky smell was manure of some type. The truck bed was bare bones, except for a bit of hay, a spool of orange twine, and the barrel on a trolley like the ones they used at the clubhouse to wheel kegs inside. The back window wasn't tinted and he spotted a horseshoe dangling from the rear-view by a length of twine. Marco got behind the trolley and grabbed a hold and leaned it back. Had a bit of weight to it. They were definitely dumping something. He wheeled it onto the tailgate and Eddy reached in and picked up the base easily, and together they lowered it to the earth. Marco climbed down from the tailgate.

"We gonna sink this thing?" said Marco, as he took control of the trolley.

"Who said anything about sinking?"

"We're in a marsh." And Cookie had told him to dress down, no point in soiling a good outfit. But Marco never dressed down. DKNY, Gucci, Hugo Boss, only designer clothes.

"Just told to meet you and dump this where it won't be found anytime soon," said Eddy. "Besides, barrels don't sink." He scratched the back of his neck, looked quickly to the right as if he heard something, then faced Marco and pointed a finger like a gun at the barrel. He squeezed off a few shots. "Unless you shoot a few holes in it." He motioned his gun toward the front of the Dodge. "There's a road twenty paces ahead on the right."

Marco leaned the trolley back and wheeled around the Dodge, hearing the tailgate slam shut. Eddy's footsteps crunched on the frosty gravel behind him. When Marco arrived at the road, he waited until Eddy caught up, and told him it was more of a path than a road. And then they headed into the marshland.

There was a wind blowing the long grass and cattails around. Marco tilted his head back. The stars and white quarter moon were bright in the sky and in a moment of wonder, he thought how beautiful it all was. Maybe he'd buy a telescope so he and Char could look at the night sky together. She liked that kinda shit.

Eddy kept his chops shut, which was fine with Marco. He didn't feel like cracking to a tool anyways, just wanted to use it to do the dirt and go home. He wheeled over a few green shotgun shells, spent. They were sixteen-gauge, and he remembered that duck-hunting season had ended a week ago. He and Cookie hadn't gone this year as they had in the past few. Cookie had just bailed out of the joint after spending a month inside—eating slop and dealing with junkies, crabs, and lice—after the cops were tipped off about an extortion job from three years back. A private car dealership owned by some Russian tool that the boys had cleaned out: cars, trucks, even two armoured SUVs headed for a sheik in Saudi Arabia, and of course real tools, a whole fucking whack of them. And while Cookie was awaiting bail, the cops raided his house, seized all his firearms. They smashed his TV and ripped the trophy heads off the wall too, just to fuck with him. The snitch would pay pounds of flesh and the boys already had a few people in mind. Maybe Marco would get to handle it, show them again what he was willing to do for their respect, for the club.

Even though the barrel wasn't that heavy, and Marco strong from lifting heavy iron in the clubhouse gym and pumping himself with roids, he began to sweat and felt his biceps and delts straining and tightening. They rounded a curve and Marco saw a fork some ways ahead and stopped.

When he turned to ask the tool which way to go, Eddy flashed those tusks so close that Marco staggered back. He let the trolley go, and the base slammed to the hard earth. His throttle snapped open again. "Why the fuck you sneak up on me like that?" he said, his voice high. Marco was about give him a shove, but he couldn't find Eddy's eyes at the back of those caves. That curbed his violent impulse. "You wanna get in my coat and cuddle you fucking weirdo?"

Eddy muttered over his shoulder, almost as if he was talking to someone, and then he pointed up the path. "Wanted to catch you before the fork is all. Let you know you can take a left." He clicked his tongue, thrusting his chin to the right. "Or you can take a right."

"Could've called out," huffed Marco. He could smell garlic again, and was sure it was coming from Eddy's mouth. "Which way's faster?"

"Oh, definitely right," said Eddy. "But it's a tougher go." He gestured to the barrel. "No problem for a desperado like you, though, huh?"

Marco bit his tongue and felt a sharp pain. Could Eddy sense fear like Marco could sense fear on others? That feeling that gave him power. He was caught in one of those rare instances where he felt like a frightened kid again, like after his parents died, when he was living with his crack-head aunty in the North End. But not actually living just existing: eating beans and white Wonder Bread from the foodbank and stealing pork chops from the grocery, wearing hand-me-down jeans with patches on the knees, shoes with the soles flopping loose, the kids all laughing at him. And him trying to sneak home after school to dodge the gangs who were always lurking around on the streets, waiting to lay a beating on a kid, steal whatever little he had. Marco was there again for a too-long sec before he got his shit together.

He jerked the trolley back and stormed forward, shoving it along the path like those angry mothers with their strollers on Welfare Wednesdays, giving the impression they'd been fucked over for their cheques, wouldn't be able to buy dope from one of his soldiers. When he reached the fork, he went right without glancing left. He slowed down after a minute and Eddy came up on his side and stayed there, every once in awhile saying, "Just a ways now." The path narrowed as they made their way until it was about five feet wide. Now and then one of them would break through puddle ice, the sound piercing the night. The marsh grass seemed to get higher, the cattails thicker and the night darker the farther along they walked, and Marco felt smaller here in the wilderness, away from the city. He thought of Cookie and Hansel handing him his patch at the ceremony, the cheers, handshakes, and hugs from the boys after. This soothed him because he knew that every step he took got him closer to what he wanted.

And, just to think, it was only a few years ago when doing dirt had scared him, really fucking scared him. It had slowly become easier and easier until he now did the acts with a detachment that Hansel told him,

31

during a club party in Calgary, signalled he was well on his way to being one of the boys. How fucked up would this look to a Joe Blow? He and the tool wheeling a barrel into a marsh, like something out of an old gangster movie: the black and whites they watched at the clubhouse, the ones with Boggart or Cagney. The ones they didn't make anymore, said Hansel, because they showed how clever the bad guys were and how stupid the fuzz was. Marco was on his way to an unknown spot, doing dirt for the boys, earning that respect from the men who'd thrown him a bone when he needed to sink his teeth into something, anything, or die on the street with all of the other scum. What was the tool doing this for? Maybe a new truck? Maybe razors to shave his chops? Maybe mouthwash to kill the garlic smell? That was it—mouthwash. Marco smiled foxy.

They carried on like that for a ways. A horn from an eighteen wheeler blared in the distance. Marco heard Eddy mutter again, then start whistling a tune softly, a tune Marco thought he recognized, but couldn't place. For sure this tool was loonier than the others.

A few minutes passed and the path widened. It sloped into a marsh with ice on the surface, white crust here and moonlight there. Marco thought it would be a good place to hunt duck. With a four wheeler, a guy could launch a small aluminium boat here. Maybe next year he'd show Cookie the spot, depending on what was in the barrel.

"This is good here," said Marco, breathing heavy, vapour coming out of his mouth.

Eddy crossed his arms over his chest, stepped to the marsh's bank. "Yup. Perfect."

"How we going to do this?" Marco rapped the steel barrel, which made an odd resounding noise.

Eddy seemed to be looking out over the marsh toward the city, his back to Marco, when he spoke: "It's a nice location. There's a lot worse places in this world. Places where bad things happen to good people, not the other way around. I used to ride bulls, you know, local shows, but stopped 'cause I broke my arm in five places." He lifted his arm and rotated it a few times. "I realized I still needed the adrenaline, so I was a rodeo clown for a couple of years, until Devil—a big mean prick of a bull—gave me a hoof to the head. Coma'd me for nine months. Run a small ranch now, fifty head of cattle, some pigs, chickens—a hundred acres that no one goes on. Take the odd job once and awhile. Me and

Jimmy." Eddy turned around and looked back the way they had come from.

"Hey, what the fuck you talking about, man?" said Marco, shaking his head. "Let's get this done."

"We'll get on with it after I piss." Eddy headed over to the edge of the grass and cattails. He began to whistle that tune again. Marco, still shaking his head, gazed at the glow above the city. He could hear Eddy pissing, whistling. Definitely loonier than the others. Char was underneath that glow waiting for him to come home so they could watch a movie. They'd sleep in until three or four, then head out for an all-day breakfast somewhere, where he'd lock her in with the diamond ring. The wind stopped and the only sound was a train trundling far off.

As Marco turned, a light flashed. He was struck on the back of the head. He felt a stabbing sensation, heard a *whoomphf.* Stunned, he tried to speak but nothing came out of his mouth. Another flash, then another. Marco tried to lift his arm but it wouldn't move, and he smelled pine dust and aftershave, the smell of his father. And then his father was standing in front of him, arms outstretched, waiting for Marco to jump into those arms so he could lift Marco up and whiskey rub his cheeks, like he always did when he came home from the furniture plant. He could hear his mother in the kitchen, too, the clatter of plates on the table. Then it was gone. And the earth rushed toward his face.

Eddy stands tombstone still, begins to sing the tune he had been whistling: "Hang down your head, Tom Dooley, hang down your head and cry. Hang down your head, Tom Dooley, 'cause boy youse about to die."

Jimmy's being is here now, no longer only a voice, and he kneels beside the bandit, who was letting out a death-rattle. He clicks his tongue as if mightily impressed. "Guess I owe you fifty," says Jimmy.

Eddy zips up his coveralls and strolls, all calm-like, over to Jimmy and nudges the bandit's head with his cowboy boot. The back is slick with blood and he sees a pool of blood forming on the cold earth, steam rising up. He clicks his tongue.

"Seventeen paces instead of fifteen," says Jimmy. "Dead-on you pistolero, you. In the dark, too."

"Had a bit of moon," says Eddy, grinning. He looks up. It is bone white and stark, shaped like a sickle blade.

"Last time I bet you. Probably swindles me. Practicing a shitload when I am not around."

"You're always around."

Scratching his chin, Jimmy grins and nods and gives the bandit's hip a kick. "Had to be the testiest little prick we ever dealt with."

Eddy unscrews the muffler from the barrel of the .22 and slips both into his left coverall pocket. He comes out with a garlic clove which he puts into his mouth and chews. He kneels down and Jimmy stands up. He begins to tug the rings from the bandit's fingers. One ring, a bull with ruby eyes, is stuck so he snaps the finger back and forth as if he is breaking a chicken leg at the knuckle, and yanks it off. He puts the rings in his own pocket, and then remembering the watch, he goes for the wrist and unclasps the gold watch there and slides it off, puts it with the rings.

"Check them pockets," says Jimmy. "Bandit's always got a little something extra."

He searches the pockets and finds a knot of bills two inches thick and he puts the knot in his pocket. Next he finds a ring box. He lifts the top and inside is a woman's diamond ring. He holds the box up and the diamond glitters in the moonlight.

"What a nugget there. Gotta be a karat," says Jimmy.

"Could be two." He snaps the ring box shut and stuffs it back in the bandit's pocket. "Bad ju-ju taking a wedding ring."

Jimmy clicks his tongue and says, "Yes, sir," and then kicks at the bandit's boot. "Never seen fancies like that. Probably worth a thousand bucks."

Eddy grabs a toe and shifts the boot back and forth. "They're too small. But they'll fit my boy in a few years."

"You always been a reasonable one, you know that."

He tugs the boots off the feet and tosses them to the side, then he reaches back into the bandit's pocket and takes out a pack of cigarettes. "Been years. How about it?"

"Why not," says Jimmy. "Something gets you, might as well be by your own hand."

Eddy stands up shoulder to shoulder with Jimmy and Jimmy reaches inside his coverall pocket and removes a book of matches. Eddy takes out two cigarettes and puts one in his mouth. He gives one to Jimmy, who sparks a match and shelters the flame with his hand and lights both cigarettes.

Out over the horizon, the light above the city hovers. Strange like a dome over one of those futuristic cities in those science-fiction comic books he would read as a boy. What did the bandit think before his lights went out? Was it nothing, just black, just black and void? Or was it like one of the nightmares Eddy had been having ever since the coma. Where a vortex sucks you down and down and rips the limbs from your body as you scream a soundless scream and you hear wails and shrieks and they build in your ears until your head explodes in a mess of skull shards and brain matter—and you think it is over but it repeats again and again until you awake in your bed, body and sheets soaked in sweat and piss.

Jimmy steps beside him and drags on the cigarette, the cherry lighting up his eyes which are as black as Alberta crude. He exhales. "Been asking yourself that question a lot lately. Sentiment doesn't suit you. Remember what the psychic said, 'Don't doubt yourself. It'll be your end."

Eddy fixes on the sickle moon until he finishes the cigarette. He butts it out on his boot and stuffs the butt in his left pocket. "You mean—it'll be *your* end." He steps over to the barrel and twists and pulls the top off and rests it on the earth. He kneels down, smelling filth, and scoops up the body like he scoops up one of his stillborn calves. He dumps the body, head first, into the barrel with the forty pound bag of chicken manure. He pretzels the legs down inside, and then lifts the barrel top and puts it on, and with the bottom of his fist, he hammers it down.

When he finishes, Jimmy is gone. Always seems to happen when there is hard work to be done. He listens for his voice, but hears only cattails pattering. Eddy picks up the boots and tosses them onto the lid. As he wheels the trolley back down the path, he thinks of the fifty thousand dollars he will pick up tomorrow from Hansel, of how he will repair his bailer before spring and patch up the steel roof on the big barn. But that is down the road a ways. Tomorrow he will pick up his kids for the weekend and they will plan a spring trip to Mexico. Cancun or Mazatlan. One of those all inclusive resorts. Swim with the dolphins. Yeah, get some photos of his kids swimming with them dolphins.

Spectacular Leo

In late August of 2012 I flew out to the West Coast to help my father die. Dying with dignity, taking control, humane euthanasia, there were so many euphemisms for assisted suicide. If I had not agreed to help he would have been in the hospital, exactly what he didn't want, and I would have been on stage—what he always wanted. He had been too stubborn to accept Ben and Rupeet's help. He fooled himself in thinking it would all go as planned. I had been fooled too. How did you plan for the unpredictable? You could prepare, but you could not plan. If anyone should have known that it was me. None of it mattered at that point. We had been on the beach for an hour. We were fully committed.

When a branch snapped behind us in the forest I turned and craned my head over the half-buried log. I thought maybe it was a cougar or black bear lurking in the shadows between the firs and cedars some thirty feet away. And maybe after seeing us awake he had decided to leave. Or maybe he was waiting until we fell asleep before he attacked— had to be a *he* if it was a flesh-eater. A woman and her dying father would be easy prey.

I searched those shadows for awhile until I decided whatever it was had left. I ran my eyes along the rock formation that stretched from the forest to the ocean where it jutted out like a natural pier, collecting a line of foam that rose with each pulse of the tide. The beach had not changed much in the fifteen years since I had last visited with my dad—horseshoe shaped, pieces of driftwood, clumps of seaweed—even the lights from Port Angeles across the Juan de Fuca Strait were as I remembered. Still, this thought didn't bring the sense of comfort and security I was hoping for. I didn't recall even an iota of anxiety or worry before, but then the circumstances were much different then and it would be like comparing hope to a death knell.

The wool blanket we were sitting on had failed to stop the sand from sucking the warmth from our bodies. And there was a wind starting to blow in off the Pacific, carrying the raw scent of briny kelp and causing the trees to groan. I rewrapped the duvet around our shoulders and hunkered us down behind the log and snuggled him like a mother sparrow nestling her chick.

He leaned forward, silent. I desperately wanted to talk to him, to hear his voice, but it would have been selfish of me to try and force conversation. Instead, I just listened for sometime as the tide flowed onto the sand and the sky's deepening purple shifted to black, awakening the half moon and stars. When a chorus of whale blows sounded our silence became too much for me to bear and I rocked him gently. "The moon and stars are out."

He stirred and tried to lift his head, as if awakening from a drunken stupor, but it dropped and he hacked and spittle drooped to the blanket. I wiped his lips with one of the filthy handkerchiefs that I had promised myself I would burn after this was all over.

"It's okay, just relax," I said. "You don't need to look. Mars, Saturn, Spica. The Big Dipper, Draco, and the Little Dipper."

He remained silent, lethargic. Hiking down the trail to the beach had wiped him out, and me, too. He had been so robust, so full of gusto, so alive when he knelt down in front of me all those years ago and guided my finger to a constellation and said, *We were born under Leo, Brianna, that's our sign. We watch him from the Earth and he watches us from the heavens.* The times we had shared here emboldened me with dreams of who I could be, possibilities, aspirations, things that sparked imaginations.

"Leo," he whispered, feeble and raspy. "Is Leo there?"

For a moment I thought I saw its stars glittering. But, only for a moment. "*Yes*, Leo's there. A spectacular Leo."

He grunted and nodded. Satisfied. Then a rumble shook the night, growing louder by the second. To the west the bright lights of a cruise ship appeared as the vessel cut through the strait toward us. He patted my arm and said, "We missed our cruise," and chuckled hoarsely.

I rubbed and squeezed his hand, which felt like dry, crinkly newspaper. We had always talked of taking a cruise from Acapulco,

Mexico, up to Anchorage, Alaska. See the coast and islands, whale watch, enjoy each other's company. My eyes moistened then and the ship rumbled past and disappeared around the small rock peninsula to the east. It was Victoria bound so the tourists could enjoy the city my dad had called home for twenty years, until today.

A minute later the ship's wake collapsed softly onto the beach, washing up bits of wood and kelp and rinsing away a stretch of our trail, every draw back the wet sand glistening. I felt emptiness in my stomach and realized I had not eaten or slept for thirty hours since I was on the plane, where I had been hounded by "Mr. NHL." Every time I had opened my eyes he was leering at me from across the aisle. A more appropriate title would have been: "Mr. I-Have-a-Tan-Line-for-a-Wedding-Band-so-Call-Me-Pig." Exhaustion was setting in and everything began to seem hopeless and uglier and warped.

Picking my dad up at his house, the drive, the hike, all of it had overwhelmed me emotionally and physically. My mind and body begged for sleep, even with the possibility that the cougar or bear—or whatever type of wild, ravenous carnivore it was—might return, attack, and then devour us both, before the arrival of our sunrise. I felt like I was falling asleep. I perked up and opened my eyes, unsure how long they had been closed. He was shaking, so I hugged him softly and asked if he needed anything. He said he wanted to lie down, to face the ocean, so I gently eased us down and cradled his bony chest and allowed my eyes to shut.

*

A year earlier my dad and I sat in Muskoka chairs beside my nana's boathouse, the new cedar siding's aroma wafting in the sultry evening. We had not had the opportunity to talk really since Milo and I arrived the night before. My younger cousins had kept me busy, asking round after round of questions: *How big was Big Ben? Enormous. What was Charles Dickens' house like? Cute. And then From Chantal: Did you meet Daniel Craig? Yes. Where? At the London premier of Quantum of Solace. What was he like? Far too serious and smaller than he looks on screen.* I thought her last question was odd because she was only twelve, but then again, Mike Myers and Jim Carrey posters plastered my bedroom walls when I was her age.

"My father and I used to sit here and watch the boaters heading home in the twilight—like we are now," said dad. "He'd tell me stories while we drank Coca-Cola. War stories, and tales of love, and sailing stories after the stars appeared."

"Every time I look at the bookcase I see him in his chair reading and smoking his pipe," I said. "How's your memoir coming along?"

"Slow." He smiled and took a sip of his Pilsner. "Thought I'd have more time with retirement. Hasn't been the case so far."

"Your students must've been surprised."

"Not as surprised as when I sung a superb rendition of Blue Rodeo's "Try" at karaoke. The campus pub had no idea what it was getting itself into by throwing me a retirement party."

I tittered.

He chuckled, and said, "Glad your audition went well."

"I hope to hear back within the next few weeks. This student loan's like an axe hovering over my head. Or like an anchor I've been dragging around for too long."

"They'll scoop you up for their stable. Foolish not to."

"I'll be happy as long as I don't have to deal with another maniac prop master," I said. "Tully the Tyrant tried to kill me—the name should have been warning enough. Everyone called me *Zena the Warrior Princess* after our clash. The politics over there were unbelievable. *And* a bit entertaining."

"Your mother must be excited?"

A mosquito buzzed my ear. I whisked it away, then struck my aristocratic pose. "You know her," I said in my English accent, "she's already informed their congregation that her daughter—*Brianna Lewis*—has just returned from London's Fortune Theatre and is the next big star at Stratford."

"She's proud of you and all the work you've done. Like me. Cut her some slack."

"But I haven't even got the call yet."

He began to speak, but coughed into his hand and cleared his throat.

"Her and Robert keep pushing me to join their church," I said.

"She can be tenacious."

"When I told her I'm *exploring* she got in a kerfuffle. I'm sure she thought of Aunt Tammy coming out of the closet."

"Always liked her. Is she still living in Spain with Jasmine?"

"Yup, I chat with Tammy on Facebook. She's doing well selling vacation homes to Germans and Russians."

"Good for her."

"Handsome beard by the way," I said, reaching to fondle his chin. "Very Ancient Greek."

He drank deeply from his Pilsner, set it on the chair's arm, then gazed out over the lake. "Milo seems like a nice fellow."

Yesterday afternoon Milo had been laughing and horsing around with my cousins, and later pleading to me with his eyes as Chantal's infatuation changed to a more tangible target. "He's kind and has a great sense of humour. And he takes his career seriously. Oh, yes, you two share a love of classic literature."

"Too bad he couldn't stay another night. Play darts with Roger and me, head out tomorrow for some walleye in Percy's Bay. You know that little bay at the end of the lake where I used to take you and your mother."

"Dad, you know how this profession is. His future depends on his reputation, and he's so close to a directorial debut," I said, giving an inch between my thumb and forefinger.

He reached over and patted the top of my other hand, which was resting on the arm of the chair. "You *sure* you're ready date?" he asked quietly.

I took a deep breath and exhaled. "It's been years, and I just can't go the rest of my life alone. This feels right."

"As long as you're ready."

There was silence between us then. After a fish jumped and splashed in front of the dock dad shook his head and smiled and tipped his Pilsner slightly toward the water and spoke: "You learned how to hook a worm here."

"I had a first-rate teacher," I said. "You always made sure to teach me tomboy lessons."

"You hooked your finger right here too, barb and all."

"And thankfully I had a very capable hook remover for a dad."

Laughter carried down from nana's cottage. Uncle Roger's accordion bleated to life and he erupted into song, hands clapped along. I twisted in my chair. Through the large picture window I could see figures swinging their arms around and dancing. My Aunt Mel, Uncle Terry, my cousins, Chantal and Bradley. And even Grandma Lewis.

As we listened to the revelry carry on I searched for constellations. "What did you find?" he asked.

"Um ... Andromeda and Pegasus."

"There's Draco and the Little Dipper. Way over there is our Leo. And right there," he pointed, "is the space station."

Six months after the family get-together I flew out to Victoria to visit my dad. We were sitting at a corner booth in Earls. I was picking at a spinach salad that I had carelessly drowned in strawberry vinaigrette, while drowning myself with merlot.

He barely ate anything and seemed to have only an appetite for Corona, which made me think his being famished had actually been an excuse so we would not have to be alone.

He asked questions about the Stratford Festival, about my understudy for the female lead and Milo's directorial debut, both for *The War of 1812*. I answered while staring at his dark sockets and bloodshot eyes neither the brim of his navy-blue Gatsby nor dark-rimmed glasses were able to hide. All the while, the patrons' prattle and laughter and the smell of cooking beef and spice was suffocating me, making me nauseous. I regretted agreeing to dine out.

When I first arrived and saw him at the airport I lost my breath momentarily. He was stooped and haggard and frail. I started asking questions, which he parried. He then said that he would explain everything after dinner. That time was now, as far as I was concerned, and I didn't want to wait any longer. I wanted answers to my questions. It would have been easier to go at him if he had pressured me for answers when I came to him in my last year of university, distraught with my secret. But he didn't. He waited days until I revealed to him what had happened: *"He wouldn't stop and I tried dad, god I tried, and he kept pushing me. I didn't know what to do. I still don't know and I feel broken inside and I don't want to feel this way anymore. Dad, I'm scared."*

"You're safe now, safe here," he said, hugging me. "How does this go? You decide and I'm with you a hundred percent."

I rested my head on his right shoulder. Across the park, a young father held an ice cream cone for his daughter as she struggled to tie her shoelace. "I just want it all to go away. Everything, like none of it happened. I'm such an idiot, I'm so stupid."

"It's not your fault."

"Not exactly, but drinking all night with the asshole didn't help."
Dad started rocking me.

"I didn't want to be questioned by the police or go to the hospital and be examined or probed," I said, and raised my head from his tear stained shoulder and looked at him. "You understand right?"

His face softened. "Bria, I don't need an explanation. Whatever you choose to do I'm with you."

And three months later, over the phone, he had listened as I told him it felt like a part of me had been stolen, like a void was there and I didn't know how to fill it, and maybe if I had went to the police, maybe I would feel different, whole again.

I took a long drink of merlot and wrung my clammy hands together under the table.

After dinner we took the stairs down to the inner-harbour's promenade where we walked along under the dull orange cast by the lamps. The boats were rocking to and fro on the waves and the docks were rolling, grinding on their pylons. I was tipsy and felt reckless.

"Let's stop a minute," he said with a cloud of steam. He wiped a black handkerchief across his mouth and nose, then slipped it into the pocket of his navy-blue pea coat, the one I had bought him for his birthday. He stepped to the edge of the promenade and placed both hands atop a waist-high post and leaned forward to rest against it. He stared out at the harbour or maybe beyond to where the fog bank merged with the dark surface of the Pacific.

"*Please* tell me what's wrong?" I asked.

He was silent as a saxophone began to wail from one of the city's clubs.

I stepped forward and clutched the chain between the posts, the cold steel biting my palms. "*Dad*, tell me."

His mouth opened and closed a few times, then he said, "I'm very, very sick."

"Is it cancer?"

"Yes."

"What type?"

"Pancreatic. But it's metastasised."

"Spread?" I asked

"Yes," he said.

Not shattering, I thought. A girl I knew at university, Beth, had been diagnosed with breast cancer, left for treatment, and returned the following year healthy. And my Uncle Roger had beaten prostate cancer. And there were a handful of others I knew that had recovered from different types as well. I exhaled and let go of the chain. The clouds were spitting; I buttoned up my collar.

"Okay," I said, nodding. "When do you start chemo?"

He fixed on the waves crashing against the harbour's breakwater, reminding me of a starved sailor in a Chekhov play: too weak to speak, or too hopeless to bother.

I grabbed his forearm. "*When?*"

Sighing, he bowed and shook his head. "It's spread to my lungs and liver—it's complicated."

"Why didn't you tell me sooner?"

"To have you worry over something out of your control?" He stepped back from the post and faced me.

"That's selfish. You should've told me."

"I didn't want you to drop your life and come here and play nurse."

"The nerve. You're going to try and convince me it was for compassionate reasons. Say it. You're dying. *Say it*. Give me at least that."

He shut his eyes and coughed into the handkerchief. I heard footsteps and a dark figure wearing a hoody strode past us and became one with the shadows and was gone. "I should've had the choice," I said. "You were never good at that, though, giving me a choice. But that's always been your flaw, your defect. Forgetting about your family at the most crucial times."

"That's not true."

I wiped the tears away with my fingertips. "So what now?"

"Well. There are plans."

"Plans? Plans? *What kind of plans?*" I said, steam billowing from my mouth.

"I'm not going to die surrounded by disease and death. I'm going to die with dignity."

"Spare me the euphemisms, you're going to kill yourself."

Then it all clicked: his unexpected retirement; the handkerchief he kept slipping out during our family reunion to tend his 'allergies'; his beard and lean face. All of it had been there, even his eyes, but I had failed to see his deliberate deception.

"You *knew* back in the summer at Nana Lewis's, even before then. How long?"

He looked toward the parliament building.

I balled my fists until my nails stabbed my palms and turned away. Condo lights shone in the dark seemingly wavering in the rainy mist. I whirled around. "I know what you're doing," I said, thrusting my finger like an epee. "You want to be the director of your own sicko performance—the tragic hero who beats fate at its own game. Choose your exit. Make it romantic."

"This *is* reality." He gestured above his head. "There's no deus ex machina dropping from the heavens to save me. I drive this bus—*me*."

"What about the passengers? What about your family? What about me?"

He was breathing heavily. "This isn't easy for me, Brianna. And I know it's not for you." He removed his Gatsby, held it to his chest, and ran his shaky hand through his wispy, grey hair.

"You already left me once," I said.

Two days later, we stood in the line-up at the departure gate in the Victoria airport. Passengers were arriving, checking luggage, and saying goodbyes. In front of us a young couple talked of their trip to Salt Spring Island, and behind us three middle-aged sisters chattered about how cozy Cook Street Village was and how it was the perfect neighbourhood for their mother. Dad and I had not spoken about his cancer or our argument on the promenade over the remainder of the two day visit. It was as if a tacit agreement had been made to stay away from the subject. Instead, we spent our time together reminiscing, which made the future seem less bleak, less urgent.

"I'll be back next week to stay for awhile," I said.

"You'll do no such thing. Ben and Rupeet have agreed to help me with anything that comes up," he said.

"Dad, please."

"Not up for debate. You have your career to think of. Nothing you can do besides sit around while I work on my memoir. Stratford needs you. Milo needs you."

"Dad."

"Brianna. You're the lead's understudy." He waved his hand away from the line-up and we stepped out, allowing the sisters to go ahead.

"Milo can replace me. There's a wealth of talent at Stratford and the show doesn't open until June."

"*Brianna*. End of debate." An elderly woman turned around and mumbled something.

Dad and I looked guiltily at each other, the pallor of his face glaring under the light. His mouth became a slash and his eyes narrowed. I had seen the same face on nana when she refused to budge while haggling at flea markets; a face that sometimes stared back at me in the mirror; a face I had seen so many times which told me there would be no changing his mind.

"Okay," I whispered, "but we keep in close contact. And promise me if anything comes up, anything at all, you'll be open with me."

He placed his hand on my shoulder and squeezed. "Of course."

I sighed and tucked a lock of hair behind my ear. It was all happening so quickly. "After the show ends in August, I'll fly out and stay for awhile. Maybe I'll ask Milo to come. He'll need a holiday by then."

"Alright," he said. "I'll be here. Ben wants to throw me a launch party. Like NASA does for its astronauts."

I tittered and covered my mouth. "Only you would say that right now."

He grinned and his eyes sparkled. It was the first such look I had seen since my arrival. From the airport's PA a woman's voice announced the boarding of Westjet's flight to Toronto. People began to file through the gate. He stepped forward and said, "Come here," and hugged me tightly and rubbed my back. "You following your dream makes me proud, and makes this bearable."

As we held each other I thought of our argument on the promenade. I thought about his decision and our last two days together. I thought about his chronic grimace, coughing spasms, the blood-specked phlegm on his lips. I had seen the prescription medications untouched in his cabinet. There was no question. He was dying. He let go of me and we stood there silently until the last person in the line-up, a young man with ear-buds in, passed through the gate.

If I said another word I was sure I would be unable to leave, so I lifted my carry-on and slung it over my shoulder. I turned and walked to the gate and handed my boarding ticket to the attendant, and a moment later headed down the jet-way.

When I took my window seat all the passengers were on the plane. The seat next to me was empty and I was glad because I didn't feel like sharing superficial pleasantries or conversations about the weather or on-flight movies and snacks. As we were instructed on safety protocols I opened my purse to search for Chapstick and found an unfamiliar brown envelope. Inside, there was a note in my dad's wild handwriting, *The axe is no more. The anchor's chain is cut. Love Dad*, and a bank draft for twenty thousand dollars.

On the morning of June 15 I was at my condo in Stratford, rehearsing lines for *1812*, when my cellphone rang.

"Brianna," said dad.

"Why haven't you returned my calls?" I said.

"It's over. I'm done. Can't wait any longer."

"I'm on my way." I stood from the chair.

"No. Don't."

"Do *not* push me away right now."

I darted into my bedroom and yanked the suitcase out from under my bed and began making a mental list of what I needed. He was silent. "Are you there?"

"I'm too weak to make it."

A month before, he had shared his plan with me. He had chosen a place we knew well, the beach by Witty's Lagoon. "Dad, I'll be there tonight."

"I'll be here," he said in a hoarse voice and hung up the phone.

Dazed, I walked out to the kitchen. All that mattered in my life was about to collide and shatter and I was not sure if I would be strong enough to put it all back together, or even if I could. My hands were shaking, so I placed my cell down on the table and sat down and looked at the *1812* script. I raked my hands through my hair and tied a loose ponytail, then picked up my cell and called my mother.

She answered. "Shouldn't you be rehearsing?"

"I need to fly to Victoria."

There was a pause. "It's your father, isn't it?" She knew he had cancer, but didn't know of his plan.

"Yes."

I heard a spoon chink in a teacup, followed by a slurp. Choral music was playing in the background, from the clock radio that sat on her kitchen counter. "Brianna. You've already done dress rehearsal. Tonight's press night for *1812*. Did you tell him Melissa broke her leg? That you're the new lead?"

"*No*, mother."

"I'm sure he would understand. Your understudy's only had a few days to prepare."

It was not going as I had hoped, but it never seemed to when they were both brought into the same equation. I clenched the phone and my stomach knotted.

"What about Milo," she continued. "What's he going to do? The press critics will *sink* his ship—and the audience. Robert and me. Our friends. And the prime minister's going to be there with his family."

"*Mother*, it's my father," I said, rapping my knuckles on the script. "What if you were sick?"

"Brianna Lewis, think of everything you've worked for. Tonight *is* that night."

"You are absolutely right. Everything I have done in my life *is* for tonight."

All I could hear was choral music, then she dragged on her cigarette and exhaled. "So that's it, you're going?"

Shutting my eyes, I pictured her sitting at her kitchen table, puffing away, sipping tea, staring up at the steel Jesus crucified to the wooden cross above the archway.

"I should've been with him this whole time," I said.

"What he's doing is *wrong*," she said in her preachy voice. "It's a sin for you to be involved. And remember, he left us."

I paused. It was something she had said. "How do you know what he's doing?"

"Well ... he told me sometime ago."

"What's sometime ago?"

She sucked on her cigarette. "When he was diagnosed," she said, exhaling. "A year ago. We discussed the whole thing. He didn't tell you?"

I sat down and lowered the phone to the table, my hold on it tightening.

"Brianna," she said, her voice barely audible. "Brianna. Talk to me. This is—"

I hung up and dropped the phone on the table and cradled my forehead in my palms. The patio door blinds fluttered, like sad and tired wind chimes, and children's laughter carried in on the breeze. When I lifted my head the script was there in front of me. I belted it viciously and it soared off the table and hit the floor in a jumble. Then I picked up the phone and dialled Milo's number and listened to the ring.

*

Small birds were twittering and chirping. It took me a moment to realize that I was awake and no longer dreaming. I wanted to go back because then I would not be feeling my dad's shallow, shallow breaths or smelling morphine and perspiration coming from his hair and skin.

The sky was amber, close to sunrise. The backpack was open and a half-empty bottle of Evian was lying in the sand a few feet away. He had done it, without anymore of my help.

I heard a patter, then a mother raccoon with two of her young scampered past on the wet beach: not exactly the cougar or bear my mind had conjured up the night before. That was when the first rays of sunshine lanced over the horizon, striking the snowy peaks of the Olympic Mountains, like a final showing for us there together one last time.

Dad rubbed my hand and whispered, "Am I dead?"

"No." I bit my lip. His face was bluish-grey like a pearl.

"Sunrise yet?" he asked.

"Right now."

"Eyes won't open … tell me."

"The sun's rays have hit the mountains. But the moon's still out."

"Stubborn … stubborn."

"Yes. It's stubborn."

"Like me."

"No. Like us—always!" I said.

I drew a deep breath and exhaled. High above the mountains a constellation—Leo—flickered the way stars do before they wane in the early dawn.

Wally's Case of the Fear

About a year and a half before the Mayan calendar predicated the world would end, I was visiting family in Nanaimo when I met Dale, the sole owner of D.N.A. Jointery, at a local home show. He had a one-man booth set up with photos of shacks he'd built, high-end renos he'd done. He was based out of Victoria and worked all around the southern island: *Anywhere real Canadian carpenters were needed.*

I was a carpenter, Canadian to the bone. Since the age of five I'd swung a hammer. And since eighteen I'd whacked up shacks, from stick-frame to post-and-beam, in six provinces and one territory. So when Dale offered to hire me on to work on a year long project in the clouds—as he touted it—I leapt at the opportunity. And two months later I moved to Victoria, which I'd heard was a hotbed for witchcraft, the occult, and other types of weird shit.

The shack was on the Malahat Mountain, a ways up off the highway. Dale and I had been driving up there for about six months before my uneasy feeling developed, and it wasn't long after when the fear burrowed into my core like a roundworm. It stirred and wriggled in my gut as we passed through Goldstream Park at the foot of the Malahat. It awoke as we drove up the highway, and by the time we entered the property's orange steel gate, just after the summit, my mouth started gumming up, my hams squirming, and my heart pounding. If Dale hit any potholes on the way up the switchbacks, my mind conjured up the image of his white Chevy van plunging off the edge and crashing down the mountainside, and then striking the highway some five hundred metres below, where it would then explode into a fiery wreck.

As a carpenter, who regularly walked beams and rafters high above sub-floors, I wasn't supposed to be afraid of heights or mountains.

That was the case, most of the time, but that mountain, that highway (the Highway of Carnage, some locals called it) had some baffling and disturbing power over me. The fear would even linger after we'd driven down the mountain, back to Victoria. It gripped me once mid-flight while on my way to visit family in Calgary. It struck me at a friend's tenth-story condo, out on the patio. It was demoralizing. And Paul Bunyan, the bobble head on the dash of Dale's Chevy, seemed to sense my fear, always mocking me with his toothy grin, as if saying, *I know your secret. I know you're scared, Wallace.* Bunyan was Dale's idol, his idea of the all-Canadian man: strong, rugged, and fearless. Dale even kept a photo of his trophy grizzly taped beside Bunyan, which irked me greatly. Although he never said it, I got the feeling Dale had it there in hopes it might bring him good luck in a future hunt.

"Can you put both hands on the wheel," I said.

"He better have my cheque," said Dale. "Or he's gonna get a blast, eh." He turned down Red Rider on the radio: Tom Cochrane was singing about a lunatic being somewhere out there. I looked out the passenger window at the mountainside, with its towering firs and cedars and craggy rock. The terra-firma on my right, over the wide-open expanse to my left, seemed to anchor me and help soothe the fear, slightly.

The van's front-end dropped suddenly and pounded into a pothole. It jumped and landed hard, the tools banging around, the ladder on the roof racks rattling about. I clutched the seatbelt across my chest and jammed my other hand against the dash like a jack to brace myself. Bunyan's head snapped back and forth, and I hoped it would just pop off—so I wouldn't have to share a space with the leering little troll anymore.

Dale hammered his palm down on the wheel. "Sonofagun," he said. He lifted his Ray-Bans and glared at me. "What's up with you? You look like you're a worm about to get hooked." He shook his head, his lips tight, as if disappointed by my anxiety. "The Titan strapped down tight?"

"Double checked it when you were in the can at Coffee Time," I said. The Titan Ladder was Dale's latest purchase: 30' extension, featherlight, and most importantly, Made in Canada.

"He's gotta fix this road up. Pack these holes, someone's gonna get hurt again. And I tell ya, I blow a Goodyear, bend a rim, anything, I'll add it to his bill." He grinned and nodded, reminding me of his idol. "Yup, even charge him for the time it takes me to drop the van off at my brother-in-law's shop. And for lunch—if he's got a penny left after this debacle."

One of the rumours that had been circulating among the contractors: Bill had run clean out of money. Renting the 5000sq. foot shack in Cordova Bay, while building the 'project in the clouds' (the highest home on Vancouver Island's southern end) must have been draining his savings faster than karaokiars draining kegs at The Waddling Dog.

Bill Thetan and his family had moved up from Los Angeles two years before, when Bill got work with some department at the University of Victoria. He was hired on to devise an ingenious way to stop the pine beetle onslaught in B.C.'s interior. From all accounts, it hadn't been going well. Much like his project, finances, and marriage—or so another rumour went.

Dale lifted his steel coffee mug, took a long drink, and then expressed the unsatisfied look I'd come to know so well since I started working for him. "If he tries to fleece me I'll start up the Husqavarna, saw the roof off his shack." The chainsaw was Dale's threat for anyone shirking on a bill. Dale swerved around another pothole. My stomach fluttered and I gasped. Hard to believe, at the start, there'd been an unspoken pride of belonging to that glorious project. A hybrid of stone, timber, and stick-frame, with it's awe-inspiring view of Brentwood Bay and the Sannich Peninsula, and on a clear day, the snow-capped peaks on the coast and Mount Baker in the U.S. The year before, the summer's dog days followed by fall's serenity kept us motivated, but then winter came and the leaden clouds and heavy rain settled in for weeks, eventually months, mixing with the high-elevation winds to form an icy maelstrom. Dale, myself, and all the other contractors accepted the miserable weather as natural and wearily plugged away. Even when the sleet felt as if it was flaying my cheeks. Even when the goings-on—thefts, acts of vandalism, 'midnight-misuse' of Bill's trailer and hot tub—took place, we shrugged them off as bound to happen on a project of that size. But when the unnatural arrived, with the return of spring, the site lost its remaining lustre. It was as if some cunning, invasive species had landed and spread across the mountainside. Instead of overwhelming and devouring native flora or fauna, it was pulling impish pranks, some almost fatal.

First, the electrician, a Pole with one hand, had lost control of his Volkswagen van when he swerved to miss a deer. He drove off a switchback. Luckily, the van ended up wedged twenty feet down against an enormous fir tree. The Pole was able to climb out, hike down to the steel gate (the only place a cellphone picked up reception), and call a tow truck. It arrived, but after it hooked up a winch to the van and began dragging it up to the road, the tow truck's engine burst into flames and sent the hood whirling down to the highway—to much honking and squealing of brakes. That wasn't all though; the flames engulfed the cab in seconds. One flame shot out as if from a flamethrower and scorched the driver's hair and face. Poor bastard. He spent a month in the Burn Unit at Vancouver General Hospital. Then there was Mrs. Thetan's nervous breakdown. Then the log posts and beams from the contractor up island were cut too short—all fifty-four of them—and who could forget the crater and wreckage (what I believe to this day was a Russian satellite). It was as if heaven itself had hurled a missile to strike the 'project in the clouds.'

I remembered something I'd meant to tell Dale. "Bill left me a voicemail Saturday night, asking if I'd been up here."

Dale lifted his lead foot off the gas pedal a bit and glanced at me. "Left me one too," he said. I caught a whiff of skunk on his breath, a regular occurrence with Dale.

"Said someone used his hot tub and trailer again," I said. "Bunch of beer cans, some underwear, cigarette butts everywhere. Like back in the spring."

"Said the same thing to me. Call him back?" Dale wheeled around a pothole.

"Too busy." Too busy swigging Molson Canadians and karaoking. "Didn't get the chance to."

"Got that sixty you owe me for gas?" It was always a buck with Dale.

"We'll have to hit a bank machine on the way home," I said.

He grunted. "Uh-huh, yes, we will."

"He took back most of the keys for the gate," I said, changing the subject. "Don't know who'd be up here screwing around."

"Just me and those drywallers from Duncan got 'em now," said Dale. "Doesn't even leave one hidden under the rock anymore." He tapped a finger against his temple, which meant he had a hunch, knew it was right, and wanted me to agree even if I didn't really agree. "Betcha them drywallers were up here messing about after last call at the Galaxy, all sauced up." He nodded. "Gotta be them."

The Duncan boys had underbid Dale's drywaller buddy from Victoria three months before, and so whenever an opportunity presented itself, Dale would attack their character: *Their quote is unbelievable. Their crew isn't experienced enough for a custom shack like Bill's. They spend too much time bullshitting about fishing and drinking and women. And their work is shoddy 'cause all the dope they smoke.*

Dale was silent, waiting for my reply.

I thought I'd feed into the lunacy. "Could be, could be."

"Sure the heck wasn't me. I was dealing with Anna's teeth. Must have only slept six hours all weekend." He crammed a finger up his nostril and began mining. "I knew they'd cause trouble."

We took the final switchback, exposing me to the drop, the last stretch to Bill's driveway. We ascended above the trees and the rising sun warmed my arm and face the way it does when filtering through glass.

"Maybe it was Carvey," said Dale. That was new: Dale changing his mind after he'd firmly staked a hunch. Must've been a sleepless weekend or maybe the toke before he picked me up was drifting his pigheadedness down the Wacky Tobaccee River.

"No, he's long gone," I said. "Probably surfing somewhere." Carvey was a damn-good full-blooded Indian plumber from Tofino. One Monday morning, while the other contractors chinwagged and drank coffee, he called me over by the porta-potty. He said there were bad spirits on the mountain and bad medicine on the way, then loaded up his toolbox into his Subaru Outback and putted out of the driveway without another word. "And he left his key with me and I gave it to Bill," I added.

We sat silently as we climbed the final stretch and pulled into the gravel driveway, where a lone vehicle was parked, a black GMC Yukon with black tinted windows, covered in dust. Dale slowed to a crawl and stopped thirty feet from the Yukon's rear. "Never seen that before," he said.

"Me neither." I pointed at the dusty license plate. "California."

The Yukon's driver door swung open and a man wearing dark aviator sunglasses leapt out and charged at us. He raised his hand like a traffic cop, his face deadpan. Dale put the van in park and shut the engine off. "What the hell is this?"

The Yukon's passenger door opened and another man leapt out, also wearing aviators. He stopped at the rear of the Yukon. Both had dark hair, crew cuts, chiselled faces, and ropey arms dangling out of their tight black T-shirts. They could've been brothers, even twins.

The driver dropped his hand and continued toward us. The passenger stood with his hands on his hips, expressionless. He swivelled his head back and forth robotically as if he was scanning the property. I spotted a tattoo on the inside of his forearm, a black insignia of some type.

"These Yanks look like undercover cops," said Dale.

"From California?" I said. "Maybe FBI?"

"Could be from a bank down there." He started tapping his temple, then grunted and shook his head like he knew for certain Bill had gone broke.

I thought Bill could've been a wanted criminal, a fraudster maybe, doubted the mob (to meek and academic), but witness protection was a possibility.

The leader cut in front of the van and arrived at Dale's door. Dale turned and gave me his do-you-believe-this look. I shrugged my shoulders. Dale wound down his window.

"You need to leave now, sir," said the driver with a twang.

Dale huffed. "I need to talk to Bill Thetan."

The driver's head tilted a few degrees and his lips twitched. "He is not present and will not return until tomorrow." He said it very slowly and firmly as if he was trying to communicate with a stubborn ass.

"You two, uh, friends of Bill's?" said Dale, removing his Ray-Bans.

"That is not your concern, sir. What is your concern is that you follow my instructions."

"I need to get paid," said Dale, his voice strained. "My bills and my workers go unpaid—it is my concern." I couldn't help but chuckle: he had only me on the payroll, fired Dougie six months before for mooching off everyone at the site—smokes, pencils, coffee from personal thermoses.

"Sir, that is not my concern."

"My name is Dale Roberts. Not, sir." Dale pointed his thumb over his shoulder to the rear of the van. "I got chains, chainsaws in the back, and a tow package on this van." Then he pointed at the house. It was down a slope to the right, so only the top of the northern gable and its clear cedar fascia was visible. "That roof we put on last month is gonna get really concerned really fucking fast if I don't get my money."

It could've been the masterful way Dale delivered the threat, or the mental image of the roof being hacked off, then dragged behind the van, or maybe a combination of the two, but when the driver spoke—after a pause—his voice had lost some timbre. "Sir, calm down and listen to me."

Dale pounded a fist on the wheel, his grey ringlets jiggling. "You listen to me. I want my final fucking cheque. Snow will fall before I leave without it."

The driver stepped back, gravel crushing underfoot. He tottered back and forth a few times, and blew from the side of his lips as if depressurizing. The passenger was still by the Yukon, but his right hand was behind his back. The saliva left my mouth and my tongue began to feel like coarse sandpaper. I nudged Dale's arm; he jerked it away.

The passenger had me worried. I remembered my aunt's tale about the grocery-store parking lot in Florida. A purple-haired grandma had slipped a small black revolver out of her garter and kneecapped a would-be purse snatcher. After, she blew smoke from the barrel. The crowd in the parking lot whooped and cheered. *You wouldn't believe the stance she took*, my aunt said, *like a cop you see in those cop shows at the firing range—part of the American culture*. If grandmas packed revolvers, I wondered about the heft behind that fit Yank's back. I settled on a chrome cannon, a .357 Magnum with a laser sight and hollow points the size of my middle-finger.

Dale's thick chest was heaving. He and the driver stared at each other like two dogs from different neighbourhoods jockeying for the same fire hydrant. Dust blew around the driveway. I felt as if I was the only sane person in that stand-off. I pressed myself against the beaded seat cover, wishing to slide in and vanish from there to anywhere.

A long thirty seconds passed before the driver glanced at his partner and wagged his head. The passenger slowly brought his hand out from behind his back.

I exhaled—struck light-headed—and realized I'd been holding my breath.

"How much is owed to you, Dale Roberts?" said the driver.

Dale cleared his throat, twisted in the seat, and went to lift the centre-consul's lid. The driver stepped back from the window.

"Dale," I said, backhanding his shoulder.

The passenger's right hand was a foot off his hip, fingers twitching. Dale froze. "Sonofabitch." He looked at the driver. "What's his problem?"

"He has no problems."

"Heck, I need to get my invoice book." Dale nodded at the consul.

The driver gave his partner another head wag, and the passenger's hand settled to his hip.

Dale reached inside the consul, slower this time, and removed his invoice book. He opened it and dragged a finger halfway down the page, then stabbed it a few times. "Here it is. Tom owes me sixteen thousand dollars and seventy-nine cents," he said accusingly, loud enough—I'm sure—so the passenger could hear. "And that's Canadian dollars."

The driver's eyebrows arched above the aviators until deep creases appeared on his forehead. A scar ran through his left eyebrow. It was then I noticed grey in his hair, wrinkly skin on his neck. I got the feeling he was older than I'd thought.

"I will return in one minute," said the driver. As he walked away, his black cowboy boots kicked up dust that swirled in the wind.

"You believe these loons?" Dale huffed. "Yanks."

The two Yanks faced each other and began to confer. The driver's back was to us, but the passenger watched the van. He nodded his head every few seconds. It was silent, except for the buzz of insects and the distant whoosh of cars on the highway below. Finally, the driver looked over his shoulder at us. He then marched to the driver's side of the Yukon. He opened the door and leaned inside so just his scrawny rear and legs were visible. The passenger stood motionless, still watching us.

Dale's thumb rapped the steering wheel as he rubbed the four-leaf clover keychain hanging from the ignition with his other hand. About a minute passed, and then the driver slammed the Yukon's door and marched toward us, chin high and shoulders back, a piece of white paper fluttering in his right hand like a white flag of surrender.

"See what big brass ones get you," said Dale.

When the driver arrived, he reached the cheque to the open window. Dale gave me his what-did-I-tell-you smile. He plucked the cheque from the driver, and pinching both ends, he tugged it twice and held it up in front of him, as if sniffing for fraudulence. The paper was light blue with shiny silver weave throughout it.

"Sir, now that you are paid I need you and your trainee to leave the property," said the driver.

"Here in Canada we call them *apprentices.*" Dale scrutinized the cheque. "The Church of Scientology. What's this? And the Fellowship Trust? Where the hell's Liechtenstein?"

"Liechtenstein is in Europe," said the driver. "I assure you the cheque is legitimate."

"Uh-huh." Dale didn't seem to buy it.

"Once your banking establishment phones to verify the funds, the funds will be wired within five minutes—no more."

"What about the time change? What if your bank's closed?" I said.

"Yeah," said Dale.

"The Fellowship Trust never closes," said the driver.

"I get screwed I'll be back up here in an hour," said Dale.

"There will be no problem, Dale Roberts."

Dale lifted up the cheque until sunlight filtered through and cast rainbow colours on his chest. He shook his head and then tucked it in beside his coffee mug on the dash. "You have a good day."

As Dale wound up the window, the driver said, "Aha, Paul Bunyan, a symbol of what America is built on." And I'm pretty sure the Yank then flashed a smirk.

Dale's ears and cheeks turned rosy. He started to crank up the window. The driver spun and walked toward his partner, a slight swagger in his hips as if proud for one-upping the loud-mouthed Canuck.

"Hey," Dale yelled out the half-closed window. The driver stopped, looked back. "When Bill shows up tomorrow tell him I want to talk to him." Dale jammed a phone-fist against his ear.

"You said he's supposed to be here," I said.

"I haven't been able to get a hold of him."

"Why'd we come today?"

"Thought he was trying to pull a fast one, like a few months back."

"Jesuschrist, *Dale*, his wife had a breakdown."

He started the engine, put it in drive, and wheeled the van around and headed down the driveway. I twisted in my seat and peered out the van's back window. The passenger cocked his head, looked directly at me. He smiled and snapped a two-finger salute, then turned around and that was when I saw it: not the chrome cannon I'd imagined, but a black automatic in a holster. "He's packing a gun."

Dale braked and glanced in the rear-view. "Come on, Wallace, that's a cellphone," he said. Then he sped out onto the road.

As we approached the first switchback, I was about to suggest that we drive back to Langford for a Hungry Man Breakfast at The Glenn Lake Pub. But I noticed Dale was fixed on Bunyan, clenching the wheel so tightly his knuckles looked like they were going to pop from the skin. I knew, right then and there, Dale wasn't finished. The Yank had crossed the line—he'd challenged Dale's manhood.

Dale tapped the brakes and wheeled the van hard left onto the narrow bush road that ran below Bill's site.

"What're you doing?" I said.

"I don't trust those two."

"You got your cheque. Let's get out of here. That Scientology's a cult," I said. "We don't want to mess with these guys. They got everyone behind them—politicians, actors, celebrities."

"Yeah, and Bigfoot stole your lunch. I'm sick of your conspiracy theories, your alien sightings and ghost stories. Those two could be up here ripping Bill off, stealing copper wire maybe. We got moral obligations here, Wallace. This is Canada. True north strong and brave."

"*Free.* True north strong and *free.* And why would they write you a cheque for sixteen if —"

Dale stomped on the brakes, jolting me from the seat. The van slid to a rocking stop, tools clattering about. He whirled at me with the look of a maniac. "I'm in the driver's seat. I'm the boss. And I don't trust those two. There's something dodgy going on up here. Guaranteed. I want to know what it is." Bunyan was bobbing in agreement. And on the radio, Neil Young was singing about rocking in the free world, which didn't feel so free right then. I could sense a brewing catastrophe that I didn't want any part of.

"Those guys are obviously Bill's friends," I said.

"Come on, Wallace, time to switch those raisins of yours for melons." He gave his disgusted look, and twisted the Vancouver Canuck's rubber wheel cover. "We're gonna have a look-see." And with that, he sped along the shady bush road, the low hanging boughs clawing the Titan and roof.

Dale had gone gonzo. I'd never seen him so worked up. A few years before my cousin, Fred, had slipped into psychosis after he smoked high-test marijuana. He was committed to a loony bin in Penetang, Ontario.

I remembered my uncle saying he had a chemical imbalance. At that moment, I thought Dale's morning toke might have scrambled his eggs.

The van rounded a bend and we emerged into a large clearing lit with sunshine. Dale slowed down. "Jesus Almighty, would you look at this."

I searched for words but none came to me. The clearing was the size of a hockey arena. To the left a high cliff stretched horizontally for about a hundred feet or so, behind it a ways, I knew, was Bill's site. And to the right, a flat gravel base ran to the forest. The van rolled smoothly without a crunch.

"That cliff's precision blasted," I said, hands on the dash, leaning forward, dumbfounded.

"This wasn't here a month ago."

"Were you here with Bill?"

He cleared his throat. "Uh, nope, by myself."

Toking up no doubt.

He pulled up alongside the forest at the far side of the clearing, and shut the engine off. We just sat there for a minute, looking around, while the Chevy's 350 pinged under the hood. I pictured Dale's brain doing the same.

"If you were down here last month, and we haven't seen any trucks come in or out during the weekdays, then this must've been done on the weekends," I said.

"Why would Bill build another shack here all closed in like this?" he said quietly. "Never told me anything."

"Maybe it's not a shack. Who'd want a shack up here without the million dollar view?" I waved toward the screen of trees.

Dale opened the driver's door. "Let's do a little snoop."

Look-see, snoop. What was next? "No. No. No. Let's go scarf a Hungry Man, put back some coffee."

He swung his legs out of the door.

"It's Monday. Betcha Amber's working," I said, stooping to Dale's primitive level.

He stopped a sec, his back to me. "Come on, we're gonna investigate." There it was—investigate!

"Come on, Dale, I'll buy," I said.

He climbed out and stretched his arms back. He whipped his head side to side, and gave a twist at the hip, farting. Then he plugged a nostril and shot out a farmer blow, like he always did when readying for work. Without even a glance back, he slammed the door and walked away from the van. I looked at the ignition: the four-leaf clover keychain was gone. Sighing, I opened the door and climbed out.

Dale and I headed toward the cliff. As we neared, I felt a dry heat radiating from it, and the sun had only been up for a few hours. By the time we arrived, I was wiping sweat from my brow. We spent some time examining the cliff, which rose up thirty feet or so, running our hands over its smooth face. Tree roots at the top were severed, some as thick as my arm. Dale said he'd never seen rock blasted without drill holes before, not even from top-notch blasting crews. I agreed and said it looked like it had been cut with a huge cut-saw, like the Stihl we used for cinderblocks or bricks or rebar. Dale scratched his chin and said no such tool that size existed.

He bent over and tried to pick up a nugget of gravel, but the base underfoot had been packed so tightly it took him a few tries to tug one loose. He muttered something as he lifted it into the light, squinting, like a jeweller appraising a diamond.

As I was about to tell Dale that my offer to buy him breakfast was a one-time deal, I spotted something in my periphery: a revolving glint in the forest.

"What were you gonna say?" said Dale.

I backhanded his shoulder, not wanting to take my eyes off whatever it was. "There's something in the forest."

"Huh." He stepped to my side. "Where?"

"There," I whispered, pointing.

Dale squinted and followed my finger. "Oh, yeah, there it is." He winged the nugget and began marching toward the glint.

I slapped my thighs and rolled my eyes: it was stupid of me to say anything. "Probably a crow with a pop can," I yelled flatly.

"Ain't no crow. Told you something dodgy is going on up here."

"It's none of our business. Forget it."

"Boohoo, Wallace," he said over his shoulder.

The gap between us widened by the second. I kicked at the base in futility, groaning loudly, hoping he'd stop, turn, and say: *You're right, Wallace. How about that Hungry Man. How about I—a married man, with a newborn daughter—ogle Amber while she serves coffee to me and all the rest of the old pervs.* But he continued on, not even hinting that he'd look back. I felt like I was on the cusp of an uncertain peril. Shaking my head, I looked to the van, then back to Dale. Then, I trotted after him. Together, side by side, we crossed the rest of the clearing.

As we arrived at the edge of the forest, the glinting object blinked out. We waited a minute. It didn't return. Dale said we needed to investigate. I said I wasn't interested. He said he'd pay me for the morning, and after I said I wasn't interested again, he said I could keep the gas money I owed him. Truth was, I didn't have it. And he knew it. He pointed to a trail and we entered the forest, Dale leading the way.

It wasn't as dark as I'd expected. There was deer scat on the ground, and the air was cool and damp and had that musty earth smell, like the canopy above had been holding in the moisture all summer. I thought the whole thing might not be too bad: a paid hike, a chance to debunk one of Dale's hunches, and maybe he'd feel so foolish after he'd offer to buy me breakfast. We didn't speak, just stalked along like hunters. A good hundred feet in, Dale froze mid-step with his back to me and pumped a fist in the air.

I froze. My nerves twanged. "What is—"

He fisted the air wildly as if telling me to shut my trap. We stood there in the shadows as still and silent as the tree trunks around us. The blurring sounds of the forest seemed to divide: some insects buzzed, others ticked; some birds twittered, others chirped. I heard the faint whiz of cars, and my heart thumping. I wondered if Dale heard it all too. Then he slowly opened his fist and gestured for me to come forward.

Once at his side, I leaned close. He pointed to the left and whispered slowly in my ear, "There's an opening with some kind of tripod tool. Like a laser level." The skunky smell reminded me I could be dealing with a man who was coming undone.

It took a moment before I spotted the tool: a stainless steel tripod which had a horizontal crosspiece fastened to the top. On each end of the crosspiece was a steel ball. "What the hell is it?" I said.

He was quiet, then said, "Japanese for sure."

We both stared at the tool, until Dale jutted his chin forward and said, "Let's go."

We headed through sixty feet or so of bush to the edge of the opening. As Dale was about to whisper something to me, a hooded figure slipped out of the forest on the other side of the opening and seemed to glide over to the tool. Dale pulled at my shoulder, and we squatted down behind a bunch of ferns.

The figure wore a red-hooded robe with gold symbols, shimmering in the sun, that ran vertically down the center. A black veil shrouded his face with two large black lenses like insect eyes. He pushed one of the balls, which was the size of a softball, and the crosspiece revolved silently a few times. Then he grabbed a hold of two tripod legs with black gloved hands. He stepped on a peg at the base of a leg. It sunk into the earth. He went on to the next one, did the same.

"Sonofagun," said Dale.

Suddenly another figure emerged from the same spot as the first. We hunkered lower behind the ferns. He wore the same getup; except a purple robe with silver symbols. He swung a black case at his side, like a briefcase only clunkier, as he joined Red at the tool.

Dale nudged me and gave a quick nod and his I-told-you-so face as if I was the stupidest man alive for doubting his hunch. I sure felt stupid, but it wasn't for my doubt. It was for going along with his cockamamie look-see, snoop, and investigation.

Leaning toward him, I said, "Told you it was a cult—let's get the hell out of here now."

"Ain't no cult," he hissed. "Couple fruitcakes playing dress-up."

He pointed to the opening. The black case lay open on the ground. Purple knelt down in front of it. Red started to lean over, but stopped and rose back up and slowly turned toward us as if he'd heard something. Dale hit the ground. I sprawled out beside him.

There were footsteps coming at us. I held my breath. If Dale couldn't hear my heart thumping before, I'm sure he could at that point, because it pounded like a piledriver in high-gear, probably sending tremors through the forest floor.

When I peeked, all I could see was Dale's curly grey mop: he'd buried his face in his elbow. I heard the unmistakable sound of a zipper, then a man peeing only a short distance from us. He tinkled the last drops, zipped up his fly, and the footsteps headed away.

Dale lifted his head.

I mouthed, *Let's go—now!*

He turned away and stared at the opening, refusing to acknowledge me. I spied through the ferns. Purple stood up and weaved a stainless steel baton above his head in a figure-eight motion. He flicked his wrist, and clicking and clacking, the baton extended to eight-feet long. There was a hissing sound as a balloon inflated from the tip, shiny silver like tinfoil, the size of a basketball.

Red tugged back his sleeve to reveal a watch-like gadget on his wrist. He touched the face, which pulsed emerald green, and the crosspiece began to revolve. The robes swayed back and forth, like they were warming up, as the tool revolved faster, whirling. Then Red stopped and danced his fingers over the gadget's face.

Birds flittered in the canopy. A funnel was forming above the tool, sucking up roughage from the earth, pulling at boughs and leaves and whipping ferns about—riffling the air around us. It reached up, lost in the heights of the trees.

Dale didn't budge. The robes began to circle the device in a sidestep, chanting. A new sound drowned out the whirl: a resounding hum as if from a struck tuning fork. The air-pressure changed, and the hair on my arms stood on end, my skin tickled. I could taste a tang in my mouth. The robes' chants grew louder; they thrust their arms up and snapped them down in some type of ritualistic dance.

Above, the branches creaked and boughs lashed against boughs. A small bird appeared from the canopy. It flapped its wings in frenzy before being sucked into the then vortex. Stars flashed across my vision, and my noodle felt as if it was swelling. Dale's hair blew about. Drool ran down his grimace. He didn't seem to notice, or didn't care: he was fixed on the chaos. The robes, tool, trees, and ferns seemed to waver and distort.

Purple broke formation, tilted his head back, and he thrust the pole skyward with both hands and roared. The silver balloon exploded into a brilliant light. I shielded my eyes with a forearm, and I swear the forest floor rippled like a wave underneath me. Dale began hyper-ventilating. I tried to look, but the light stung my eyes. I heard a crash behind me. The light blinked out. The whirling ceased. The air calmed. All instantly.

Then shrieks erupted. I opened my eyes. The robes were charging toward me. Dale had abandoned me, fleeing. Stupefied, I scrambled to my feet and careened through the forest in the general direction of the Chevy, ducking limbs here and there, ploughing through brush I was too stunned to avoid. Dale was nowhere in sight. I heard feet pounding the earth: the robes were closing in on me. So with my arms pumping, I opened up into a full-out work-boot sprint.

When I spotted the van, its engine roared and rear tires tore at the hard pack. A hail of gravel zinged and zipped into the forest, shredding undergrowth and ricocheting against trees. A thwack resounded behind me, followed by a yelp and loud rolling crash. I burst from the trail as the van shot forward. I leapt recklessly at the backdoor. And my right hand—with its iron grip from years of wielding a 24 oz. Eastwing, clenching a karaoke mic, and swigging Canadians—snagged the door handle, barely. The van ripped across the clearing, dragging me bouncing and flopping. When Dale slowed to take the bush road, I reached up with my left and grabbed the other handle, crying out, and hauled myself onto the bumper. I turned back. Red was in the center of the clearing, karate kicking the air and swinging around his baton— royally fucking pissed.

Dale barrelled along the bush road, tools knocking around inside the van. I struggled to hold on to the handles as we whooshed under the canopy. I felt like an unwanted passenger, like a bush tick on a donkey's ass.

Thirty seconds later, Dale braked and cranked hard left and fishtailed onto the gravel switchback, into the blazing sun. My shoulder slammed into the van's door, my foot slipped from the bumper, and my work boot dragged until the gravel yanked it off my foot. The wool sock went next.

The van's rear-end tamed. Dale gunned the engine. I had two choices: join the boot and sock or hang on and hope I didn't end up dead in a heap of mangled carnage. I sunk down and peered through the dusty back window. Dale was leaning over the wheel. I yelled his name once, then again. He didn't respond. Not daring to loosen my death grip, I head-butted the window twice. He glanced back. He didn't look shocked to see me clinging to the back of his Chevy. Then he screamed for me to hold on—the potholes!

The front-end dipped, jumped, and we soared. The rear-end bucked. I heard a loud rattling and grating noise overhead, and ducked just as the Titan snaked off the racks and clattered onto the road, where it skidded out of sight in the dust.

I head-butted the window and yelled that he'd lost the Titan.

He turned and shouted, "Fuck the Titan."

The tough, take-no-crap, great-white hunter of elk, wolf, and trophy grizzly bear, had lost his brass ones—his melons—and come unglued in the heat of battle.

When I shut my eyes, they stung so fiercely I was forced to keep them open, exposing them to the soothing air, as Dale gunned, braked, and fishtailed down the switchbacks. Not sure how long it went on for, but finally the wheels locked and the van slid to a rocking stop, enveloped in a cloud of dust thick with exhaust fumes. I heard a large truck whiz by, a smaller vehicle, then another. We'd made it—alive—to the orange steel gate and highway.

The driver's door creaked open. Boots crushed on gravel. I released the handles, stepped off the bumper, and limped to the passenger door. Dale was hunched over at the steel gate, working the lock. I climbed inside the van and sat down. "Hotel California" was playing softly on the radio.

Dale pushed the gate open, hobbled to the van, and lifted himself into the driver's seat and slammed the door. He pounded the gearshift down into drive, clunking the tranni, and stomped the gas pedal to the floor. The van ripped down the last bit of gravel road and hit the paved highway, the back end crabbing.

"Okay, okay, you alright, Wally?" he said, breathing heavy. He kept glancing in the rear-view as we ascended the Malahat, oncoming traffic flying past us.

I tried to crank the window down with my right hand but felt a sharp pain as if I'd reached into a fire. My hand was red and swollen. Wincing, I used my left to lower the window a foot.

"Wally. Wally," said Dale. "Talk to me buddy." I turned to face him. His eyes had a squirrelly look, blood spots in the whites of them. I dropped the visor to look in the mirror. Mine were the same. Vertigo struck me then, and I hunched forward and barfed onto the floor, coating my bare foot.

Dale was silent.

When I rose up and wiped my mouth, Bunyan's head was whipping back and forth. He was ridiculing me with his toothy grin as if he'd watched the whole spectacle, as if he'd been gleefully fucking entertained by the speed, screams, head-butts, and Dale's rebuffs.

I raised my good hand high, then thundered it down on Bunyan's head. Once. Twice. And a violent third time. He seemed unfazed by my pummelling, so I wrenched his head clean off and hurled it out the window. I grabbed Dale's trophy grizzly photo and out it went, too.

Dale didn't even tap the brakepedal. "Jesus, Wally, what the hell? I'm pissed off. I lost the Titan, man," he said, thumping his chest with a fist.

I shut my eyes, leaned back against the beaded seat cover, cradling my injured hand. We were silent as we crested the summit, and it wasn't until we were descending that I opened my eyes again and gazed out the window at the Earth.

The morning after, I stood out front of my apartment at the end of the sidewalk. I wore a pair of cheap sunglasses. Sometime during the night—while I rolled around in bed, sleepless, brain rippling and wrist throbbing—heavy grey clouds had replaced the clear skies.

Dale was wearing his Ray-Bans when he arrived to pick me up. And as I climbed into the van, I noticed Bunyan's remains were gone. I couldn't help but grin. We drove silently to Glenn Lake Pub, shell-shocked, like two grunts the morning after a vicious battle.

Dale bought the Hungry Man breakfasts, not even glancing at Amber as she served us. Afterward, over our third coffee, he told me apologetically that he needed to let me go. He took out a folded cheque from his breast pocket, for wages owed and a month's severance pay, and handed it to me. I guessed it was his way of ensuring the terrifying event would be buried, and with that, he wouldn't be reminded of the tragic unravelling of his prized—and flawed—idea of manhood.

Over the following week, I replayed the entire event over and over as I sipped on Canadians and nursed my migraine and sprained wrist. I figured Dale's cowardly act and our flight down the mountain had somehow liberated me from my case of the fear. And just to prove *my* hunch right, I drove that highway a dozen times, even slowing down when I passed the orange steel gate.

My case of fear has yet to return.

A Gardener by Choice

Willy finished worshiping the sun—the only God he trusted—and rose up from his knees and swiped the dirt off his trousers. He'd been watching through the chain-link fence for sometime, feeling its warmth efface the coolness of early morn as it climbed above the eastern horizon. How many years had he performed this ceremony? Did it matter?

Since he'd been condemned to die in prison, Willy disregarded time. He viewed it as insignificant as the days he'd walked as a free man, as the family he longed for but never held, and as the thousands of vacant faces he'd seen since his arrest.

Unrepentive Bank Robber Pays with Mortal Days, read the headline in the newspaper. Willy's co-accused, Nathaniel Grigs, had testified against him for a reduced sentence. He didn't mind though. Up until that point, his life had been a cycle—fear, crime, arrest, and relief. Just like that, so he'd gotten used to it.

On the clement breeze, wafts of rose were mingling with lavender and somewhere small birds were twittering. He smiled and thought how swell life was right then. Heck, it had been for thirty, forty, perhaps fifty years now. He shut his eyes, inhaling deeply, and tilted back his head until the sun shone full on his face. He basked a moment and then headed off to work, work, work.

Willy meandered around the prison's grounds throughout the morning, stopping here and there to yank weeds from the dry flowerbeds and cracks in the asphalt. Whenever he passed by other cons or guards, he refused to acknowledge them. They were distractions he didn't need this early in the day. As always, his mind gradually slipped into a utopian drift: remembering the past while revolving the present without *ever* thinking of tomorrow. No visitors, phone calls, no letters. That was how he'd managed to keep it together over the years.

How foolish the other cons were for shirking their gardening duties, he thought. Not him. *No, sirree.* He remained committed—the only one—for all these years. In the beginning, he too disliked his position as gardener, but as the days, months, and years bled together he found solace in the role. He worked in the day. Dreamt in the night. And existed *somewhere* in between. You see, he'd attained in prison what he could never get in the real world—to feel safe, because that was all he'd ever yearned for. Not abandoned by his mother. Not starved and beaten by his drunken father. And not deserted at St. Christopher's Orphanage where the boys punched and kicked him and the priests flogged him with straps until his flesh wept blood. He'd learned to fear the world more and more every year.

Hours past, with Willy's God rising high, and when he arrived at a rectangular flowerbed by the infirmary, he heard a distant siren warble on the breeze. He lifted his hand and hooded his eyes. Over the coils of rusty razor wire, quivering atop the fence, and beyond the forest of maples and pines, Willy spied a vast metropolis of concrete and glass and polished steel.

A shiver raced up his spine and bile rose from his gut; he spat at the earth. He'd witnessed this metropolis evolve and spread every year since his arrival as if it were some invasive weed choking out the landscape. He shook his head and vowed—once again—to never so much as peek at it. Scowling, he hunched over and tore a stinging nettle from the earth and tossed it over his shoulder.

Come sunset, he found himself roaming toward the prison's graveyard. A sanctuary he knew well. He'd buried friends there, and one day he would join them. For this reason, he maintained it with sacred pride, and as he passed through the wrought-iron gate, his eyes began to water. Crows cawed from their perch on the digger's shed and the weathervane atop it. Willy hobbled to the north-eastern corner. He stooped and began to weed rue and rosemary around a headstone amongst the many others that were forgotten, as all the men were underneath them.

As he finished up and prepared to move to another, he heard a voice jabber behind him, so he spun around. Loony Sam, an old-safecracker he'd known forty, fifty, maybe sixty years now, glared at him with rheumy eyes as if looking right on through him.

"Startled me *good*, pal" said Willy, brushing the dirt from his hands.

Sam clawed his rusty-white beard.

"Thought you dusted out," said Willy. "Ain't seen you for awhile." Sam's face was deadpan. Willy continued, "I should've known you'd kick off here. Once a fella been in a long while—nowhere else to go. No family. No friends." Willy waved toward the metropolis. "Besides, it's scary out there."

Sam slowly raised his arm and pointed west. A recollection lurked on the edge of shadow in Willy's mind—he refused to look west. Sam grinned wickedly as if privy to an unspoken jest. He then shrugged his shoulders and turned, and as he limped away, he began to hum a tune of sorrow.

Willy trembled as Sam departed. Glancing around, he searched for a distraction—a person, something, anything to preoccupy his thoughts so his swell day of gardening wouldn't be ruined. And then deafening booms—three in rapid succession—pounded the air like a cannonade, tousling his hair, sucking at his eardrums. He dropped to his hands and knees like a bag of manure tossed from a trailer. An odour of fetid earth walloped him good and he snapped his head back. The crows had launched into the air, kicking the weathervane into a spin. They orbited in a swarm, then swooped at Willy. He ducked. They soared up and over the razor wire and shot toward the forest.

There was a tang in Willy's mouth and the hair on his neck and arms bristled. He spotted a purplish cloud in the east billowing and rolling swiftly toward the prison; he scrambled away over the plots like a whipped mongrel about to get another dose. The cloud rolled overhead and darkened the Earth as it blotted out the last sliver of sun.

Willy stopped and rose up on his knees, tottering side to side, and jammed the palms of his heels into his eye sockets. Then he thrust his outstretched hands skyward. Moaning, searching, calling for his God as if an abandoned parishioner pleading for a miracle he knew would never come.

"Hello, William."

Gasping for breath, Willy whirled around. Jessop, a bull he'd known for a *long, long* time, stood behind him. Even in the cloudy twilight Willy's rictus reflected in Jessop's sunglasses. Hanging his head, breathing deeply, Willy surrendered to the circumstance he now understood. "Is it time?"

"Reckon so," said Jessop. "Did a *fine* job today."

"I love to garden," said Willy, looking up, trying to compose himself.

Jessop gestured a hand westward. "Maybe you oughta leave. Get the hell out of this place. Go, be at peace."

Willy gazed to the sprawling metropolis with its flickering lights, to the towering edifices of glittering glass and steel, and to the alien automobiles racing along arteries intertwined in bizarre patterns. He saw an otherworldly ritual he could neither grasp nor wish to in its profound complexity and reverence for an existence which had forsaken men such as him.

"No, Jessop. I'll stay. It's safe here."

Willy then brushed away the dirt from a lichen-covered headstone. And with his forefinger, he traced the grooves of the epitaph:

WILLIAM TANNER HOLDSWORTH
1900-1979
A GARDENER BY CHOICE.

The Promise

In 1990 my father was peacekeeping in the Golan Heights, while I was enjoying the tail end of a yearlong stay at my grandparents, Croft's Cove, on Otter Lake near Parry Sound. And it was during the last week of August that Uncle Tommy and I were out fishing in his old red and green rowboat. My bobber had been floating off the bow far too long and was lost somewhere on the lake's shimmering surface. We had been on the water since the loons had heralded dawn and already had one smallmouth bass on the chain fish stringer draped over the gunwale. My bass. Tommy was dead set against heading home to Croft's Cove until he caught one: we needed at least two for a pan-fry lunch. He sat erect at the stern, fixed on the calm water of Percy's Bay as if he were the captain of his own fishing boat on Lake Ontario, which he spoke of often.

Although not truly my uncle, Tommy was one of those distant relatives linked by a stringy chain only Grandpa Williams could remember. Fifteen years older than grandpa, he had fought in WWII. After that he and grandpa had fought alongside each other in the Korean War and spent years together in the Canadian Airborne Regiment, making them closer than blood.

"Keep your eyes open. It doesn't *feel* right here," said Tommy. His harelip and missing teeth made him sound as if he were whistling through a busted harmonica. He had been born with the harelip, but the missing teeth were the result of a hard parachute landing.

I nodded as I always did when he said he had one of his feelings.

And then he hollered: "*Pull it up. Pull,*" and thrust a finger toward the fish stringer. Something underneath the water jerked violently on it, rocking the boat. I lunged and clutched a hold of the chain, rocking the boat even more. A fierce tug-of-war ensued with an unseen opponent just below the tea-coloured water. Back and forth, back and forth. Whatever was on the end was a good size.

Fish bat in hand, Tommy scrambled to the portside, seized the chain from me, and heaved the stringer into the boat. On the end, our plump three-pound smallmouth bass, half our soon-to-be lunch—had had its soft underbelly ripped open.

"*By thunder,*" said Tommy. He leaned over the gunwale and teased the fish bat back and forth, scanning the surface.

"I couldn't see it. But it felt big, though, really big." I reached my arms out as wide as they would go. "Maybe a muskie."

Tommy shook his head and huffed, like always when angered by someone else's actions he thought inadequate.

There was a trail of bubbles heading out toward the bay's mouth, to the deeper water of Otter Lake. Tommy's eyes narrowed as he sat down, stringer in one hand and fish bat in the other. The bass dangled between us like grandpa's plumb bob, guts hanging a few inches below its half-eaten tail fin. Tommy looked at the bubbles. "Bonesaw," he said quietly, almost reverently.

An elusive monster that had been haunting Otter Lake residents for generations had struck again: Bonesaw, the giant snapping turtle. The Ojibwas from Parry Island, who sold what my grandma called junk at the local church sales, said Bonesaw had been an evil chief who had been transformed by a trickster. Grandpa called him a leviathan. One afternoon, while grandpa was marking his property line, he spotted Bonesaw on the shore devouring a log of a catfish. He managed to tag him with orange spray paint, a long stripe down the center of his shell so all the grandkids would see him coming and get out of there lickety-split.

"Nothing left, eh," I said. "Geez, I tried but he had a good hold of it, Uncle Tommy, I swear."

Tommy turned and glared at me, his face reddening, and said, "You just want to get home and see that little neighbour girl, don't ya? Eleven years old, you should be more worried about establishing a work ethic."

There had been a swelling anticipation that morning to see Melanie. So I guess Tommy's "feelings" were accurate on occasion. He opened the stringer's hook, slid the hook from the bass's gills, and hurled the fish at the trail of bubbles. "Take it, *bugger*. Bloody thief." He pumped his fist wildly in the air, as if he was wringing a chicken's neck. He muttered another oath that I could not make out and grabbed his rod and began winding in line. I did the same without a peep, because in the Williams Clan—in times like those—if you valued your hide you remained quiet. Attempts to console, soothe, or jest were considered treasonous.

When Tommy's bobber and empty hook popped over the gunwale, he huffed and tossed his rod down with a clatter. I set mine down and assumed my position as loyal first mate and navigator, remembering Uncle Tommy's promise: If I did a good job, he would gladly take me on to fish Lake Ontario after he bought his boat. He swung the oars out and plunged them into the lake and rowed toward the mouth of Percy's Bay.

As we left, a mother teal and her ducklings entered. She quacked and circled them, darting in here and there to poke them into formation with her bill as they bobbed like corks, struggling against the waves. I wondered if Bonesaw had spooked the mother and her brood and they were now seeking the bay's safety. From the other kids around the lake, I had heard the stories about ducks and beavers being taken, heard a summer family had lost their cocker spaniel after she swam out to retrieve a Frisbee. She was pulled under. It seemed as though anything with a heartbeat was unsafe in the water when Bonesaw was on the hunt. The oars grinded and knocked in the oarlocks and the water swooshed rhythmically as we rowed for homeport like sea rovers without plunder.

Come noon, I was sitting at my grandparents' oak kitchen table. My grandma, an amazon of a Métis woman, stood at the kitchen sink, towelling dry a plate. Her helmet of freshly curled hair glistened purplish in the sunlight filtering through the window. From my aunt's room down the hall, there was muffled music. She had been holed up in her bedroom for two days instead of ripping around and smoking with her boyfriend. He was a long hair named Tim with an earring and a fire-engine red Pontiac Trans Am. I had heard her caterwauling on the phone one night, telling Tim she was not feeling the whole-move-to-Brampton thing. I would often listen at the base of her door on my hands and knees. It was a gold mine for gossip. To think of it now, I learned more about teenage angst and pop icons in a year listening at her door than all of my years in high school combined.

"Why's Aunt Rosie grounded?" I asked as I peeled crust off my bologna sandwich.

"Mind your *nose*," said grandma. "Always want to know everything about this and that. You're too smart for your own good. You should eat your lunch, never mind gum-flapping."

The second hand of the lighthouse clock on the windowsill ticked slowly, slower than usual—I was sure—as if time itself wanted me to suffer in misery. The anticipation that day as I waited for dusk was overwhelming. My hand darted out and spun the Lazy Susan on the table, sending the salt and pepper shakers tumbling. I quickly grabbed them and stood them back up.

"Ants are fierce in those pants of yours today. I guess fishing wasn't enough." She pulled the drain plug. "And eat your crust this time."

Duke, my aunt's German Shepard with bad hips and one milky eye, brushed against my thigh, his tail thwacking the table leg. I smiled and said, "Yeah, grandma," and slipped the crust under the table to Duke. He snorted and woofed it from my hand too loudly. I wiped drool from my hand onto my jeans.

Grandma whirled around, her curls quivering a moment. "Doesn't mean feed it to Duke either, *brat*. When your plate's as bald as your Uncle Tommy's head, you can use some of your energy to cut coupons—IGA and Giant Tiger fliers came in this morning." When she continued, it was in her sweet old lady voice she deployed at garage sales and auctions: "Later you can give grandma a foot massage with her peach lotion. I think I have a bit of change in my purse."

Duke's tail thwacked my leg a few times and he nudged my thigh with his snout and then scrammed. "The people moving in have kids?" I asked.

She was leaning against the counter, the green dishtowel slung over her shoulder. "Not that I know of."

"No boys *or* girls?" At that time, the thought of being replaced as Melanie's best friend was devastating to my young, fragile ego.

"No children whatsoever." She smiled slyly and tapped her fingernails on the counter. "That reminds me. Why was the back door open the other morning when your grandfather got up for work?"

"Back door?" I tried to think who I could pin it on: Uncle Tommy tanked up on homebrew? Aunt Rosie? Duke? "I don't know," I said, looking down at the bowl of tomato soup as if looking at it might somehow rescue me.

At six-thirty p.m., I stood halfway up the concrete steps, waiting impatiently for grandpa to return home from his job at Ontario Hydro in Brampton. Grandpa, Uncle Tommy, and I had built the steps last August when I first arrived. There were forty-seven. They climbed up the Canadian Shield bedrock, which formed a natural amphitheatre behind the house, to the driveway above. *An engineering marvel that rivalled the St. Lawrence Seaway and CN Tower*, Tommy would always say after a few of his homebrews.

Three quick honks blared from the driveway, signalling my grandpa was home. I bolted up five steps and clicked my heels together and slapped my hands against my thighs. The truck door creaked open and slammed, and a moment later, grandpa's hat appeared at a rakish angle over the crest followed by the man himself. He wore a maroon T-shirt with the yellow Airborne Regiment's parachute and wings insignia on the chest. We locked eyes. He smiled and nodded, and so did I. He marched down the steps swinging his metal lunchbox at his side. That scene replayed daily, like a ceremony, during the year I was there, even on the dark, snowy winter nights.

"Hey, grandpa," I said, my voice echoing off the bedrock.

"What's going on buckshot?"

I preferred buckshot to brat or dear or even my real name, Brandon. I zeroed in on the lunchbox, covered in stickers of military regiments, and headed up the steps to greet him.

"Here's a treat for you," he said, hugging me close, rustling my hair with his free hand. I smelled the Old Spice aftershave, a persistent smell that clung to him even after a dip in the lake. He passed me his lunchbox.

We began down the steps, side by side. "See any trophy bucks on the road?"

"Not today. A racoon on Highway 69 almost got hit by an eighteen wheeler. That's it. Catch any fish?"

"Caught a three pound smallmouth in Percy's Bay. But Bonesaw ripped it to pieces. Right off the stringer."

He shook his head. "What'd I tell you?" He said, nudging me with his hip.

"*Keep the fish in the boat and your toes out of the water,*" we both said and laughed.

I stopped on the stairs and turned to face him. "I'm gonna miss Otter Lake when you guys move. All the fishing and swimming and the forest."

He looked down at me. He patted me on the back, which seemed to get harder every week. I figured it was his way of toughening me up a little.

"You can come back to the lake one day. Maybe even Croft's Cove," he said in a soft voice, rare for him. Even though he had never said it, I knew he did not like the idea of moving to Brampton. But the steps had been giving grandma's knees trouble, especially in the winter, and the daily commute between Otter Lake and Brampton was leaving grandpa exhausted. Out the door at five-thirty, not home until six-thirty or sometimes closer to seven. Dinner. Then snoring away in his recliner-chair until grandma woke him up and led him to bed.

After several more steps together, I broke formation and sat down, plunking the lunchbox between my legs, as grandpa continued down to the house. I unfastened the latches and flipped the lid open. As always, two plastic-wrapped mints lay at the bottom amid shrivelled mandarin peels. I squirreled the mints into my pocket for my meeting later, and closed the lid and latched it shut.

"I'll see *you* at the dinner table in a few minutes," grandpa said, his voice its usual firm tone. He stood at the screen door, watching me. Dinner was a serious affair to my grandpa. After all, the patriarch of the Williams Clan had an image to maintain and clan custom—stretching back generations—to uphold.

"*Yes, sir.*"

He smiled slyly the same way grandma did, as if they had shared it so many times over the years it had become identical. "Be careful. Don't want those mints to melt in this heat." He winked and went into the house.

I had first caught a glimpse of Melanie while building the stairs. Like an intrigued doe, she had been spying on us from behind the big maple. It marked the entrance to the deer trail which led to Otter Lake Marina. Melanie and I had met in Ms. Beasley's Grade 6 class at Foley School a week later. That fall she showed me around the forest on our side of lake, and come winter we tobogganed and built snow forts and snowshoed and drank hot chocolate her mother had made with the little marshmallows. Over the spring and summer, we ran the trails. It seemed everyday we came upon new discoveries as the woods awoke from its wintry hibernation. Intricate spiderwebs and hidden rabbit burrows, caterpillar nests the size of pup tents, bucks and does with their fawns nibbling greenery, foxes and possums scurrying about and garter snakes slithering under deadfall. As the months progressed and the buds sprouted into leaves, the woods became darker, the sunlight fighting to filter through the canopy. It became richer too, so much so it smelled and tasted lush, like I imagined the jungles were that I had always dreamt of exploring.

We solved mysteries together—the slaps on the lake that turned out to be a beaver's tale, the rusty ten-speed hanging from a tree that had once belonged to the son of the husband and wife who owned the marina. And there were unsolved mysteries—who had built the old lean-to and left the red mouldy sleeping bag inside? And what made the loud thrashing noises we occasionally heard at dusk? Other times we sat and shared family stories or dreams we had had the night before, dreams she always seemed to understand the meaning of. She was everything I wanted to be, the opposite in every way of the authoritive and disciplinary life of the army base.

When grandpa yelled that dinner was ready, I picked up the lunchbox and took the steps down to the house.

After dinner, after my bath, and after grandma's peach-lotion foot massage, I crept through the house and did some recon. In the basement Uncle Tommy was drinking his homebrew, strumming and whistling along to Gordon Lightfoot's "Wreck of the Edmund Fitzgerald." My aunt was in her bedroom talking hush-hush to Tim on the phone, and from her murmurings it sounded like they were hatching a plan to sneak out and attend a party across the lake. I crawled down the hallway to the TV room where I poked my head around the doorframe. Grandpa was nodding off in his recliner chair, snoring. Grandma was sitting in her chair knitting and humming away to *Anne Murray in Concert*, which was on the TV. When I saw her rosy tenderized feet shaking along to the music, I shuddered. They had to be the biggest feet ever maintained by child labour.

Satisfied I would not be missed, I tiptoed into the kitchen. Duke was lying under the table. He perked up and fixed on me with his good eye. I ordered him to be quiet and treated him with a slab of leftover ham from the fridge, to much tail thwacking. Then I slipped out the back door into the twilight and bolted up the steps. Halfway up, I cut left and darted across the bedrock, and when I reached the big maple, I stopped and hunkered down in the undergrowth to catch my breath. I scanned the house. The only light on was my aunt's. In my grandparents' bedroom window, I thought a shadowy form moved and the curtain swayed briefly as if someone had been there watching me. I stayed like that for awhile, listening to my heart thumping, expecting the outside lights to burst on, for the door to swing open, for grandpa or grandma to start yelling my name. Nothing happened. Then as I was about to leave, the door opened inch-by-inch and my aunt slipped out. With one hand on the knob, the other on the wooden panelling, she gently eased the door shut without a sound. She bounded up the steps, her red mane fluttering behind her like a Canadian flag in the wind. I had never seen her move so fast. It was as if she was running from one of those psycho-killers in the horror movies she and her friends always tried to get me to watch, so they could put nylons on their faces and scare the bejesus out of me. A moment later she disappeared over the crest of the driveway. An engine rumbled to life and a car slowly drove away, as if trying to be as quiet as possible. Tim's Trans Am.

I stood and began hiking along the trail, as sure-footed as a young buck, heading toward my destination, breathing in the wild air. Blocking most of the moonlight, the canopy swayed and creaked in the light breeze. Shadows were shifting about on the ground. It was not long before my eyes and ears adjusted to the dark woods. It was as if another world existed there at night—bats fluttered above, critters creaked and croaked and fireflies sparked to life and weaved amongst the bows. Something scurried through the forest off to my right and I thought of the porcupine that had taken Duke's eye with a quill.

A few minutes later, I emerged at the spot: the small clearing that overlooked the waters of Croft's Cove. On the opposite shore, the second-story light remained on in my grandparents' TV room. Melanie was sitting with her back to me on the large rock that jutted up from the earth in the center of the clearing, her glistening black hair in a

French braid. She pointed up at the sky, without turning around. "It's like a claw," she said.

The tendrils from a purple cloud looked like clawed fingers grasping at the bright yellow-red moon, not yet quite full. That was exactly why I liked her so much—because her ways seemed magical to me. She was not like the tom-boys back at C.F.B. Petawawa, playing marbles or G.I. Joes or soldiering with us boys. I scampered up the rock and sat beside her, wondering if she would hear my heart, which had not calmed since I left the house.

She turned to me. "I didn't think you would show." She wore her blue pyjamas, the little white sheep on them. She hugged her knees to her chest.

"Grandma needed my help." I hoped the peach-lotion residue on my hands would not give away the exact kind of help.

"Dad says the people moving into your grandparents' house are nice." Her father was the real estate agent who had listed and sold the house.

I picked up a twig and tied it into a knot. "They got any kids?"

"No, I don't think so."

"No boys?"

"No boys or girls, silly." She giggled.

"That's too bad." I tossed the knotted twig down the bank, and a bullfrog began croaking.

She leaned back. "When are your parents coming to get you?"

"Dad's stuck peacekeeping in the desert for another four months. Making sure Syria's tanks don't attack Jerusalem. So mom's picking me up on Sunday."

"Dad says peacekeepers got a tough job."

"Yeah, grandpa says that same thing all the time. It's dad's third tour."

"Will this be the last time we see each other."

I thought I heard Tim's Trans Am growling in the distance, maybe racing around the lake road. "I'll visit when I get my license. But we can meet up tomorrow."

"I can't. A birthday party—my parents' friend." We were both silent a moment. "Promise you'll come back when you get your license?" she said, her voice high.

"Promise I will." My voice was higher.

She waved her arm up at the night sky. "The moon looks like a peach."

I wiped my palms on the rock, gave them a quick secretive sniff. The moon had brightened and the stars were sparking to life, like those fireflies I had seen on the deer trail.

"I never saw any of this 'til you came," she said.

"It'll still be the same after I leave. You can still come here."

"Not without you." She said it in a way that made me believe her.

We sat quietly for sometime while a bullfrog croaked and the waves lapped on the pebble-strewn shoreline, pine and elm boughs swaying in the breeze. When the bullfrog silenced, I leaned forward. Something had surfaced ten feet off the shore, like a hooked submarine periscope; it turned one way and then the other.

"Look," I said, pointing at it, unsure of what it was.

After a minute, of what seemed to be recon, the periscope headed toward us, bobbing back and forth, and then a turtle shell breached the waves. I spotted a stripe of orange paint down the center of its dark glistening shell as it crossed the moonlight—Bonesaw.

Instinctively, I leaned back and so did Melanie. I hoped the shadows cast by the woods would conceal us as Bonesaw crawled onto a small strip of flat shoreline. Grandpa and Uncle Tommy had described him before, but this was my first sighting. Larger than Tommy's beer cooler but smaller than the rain barrel behind the house, his domed shell had rows of bumps and a jagged edge. Opening his hooked beak wide, he lifted his head and groaned and drummed his tail against his shell as if announcing his arrival to the wood's inhabitants.

Melanie's mouth hung open. I brushed her arm and placed a hush finger over my mouth.

Bonesaw dug a hole on the shore with his claws and beak. Then he climbed out of the hole and spun around and moved from side to side, groaning again. A little head suddenly popped up, then another, and then another until a dozen or so turtle hatchlings were scrambling from shell fragments and sand. Once at Bonesaw's side, the hatchlings sprung up on their legs, their heads high, like soldiers ready to march. Bonesaw crawled off under a pine bough into the shadows, trailed by the hatchlings, single-file until they all vanished one by one.

"Bonesaw's a mother," Melanie whispered.

"Let's keep it a secret like our spot."

"Like your promise."

As more stars flickered to life in the purple sky, the moon we had found splendidly new bathed us in its glow. I had an indefinable feeling that I never felt before, sitting beside her on that rock, as if something deep inside of me was awakening for the very first time.

Digging into my pocket, I said, "Have a mint."

She reached out her hand, tilting her head and smiling.

I handed her one.

And she said, "Why do your hands smell like peach lotion?"

Bagpipes to Freedom

Their souls have gone on to that Heaven of light
Still the echo comes back to us –
'Fight the Good Fight.'

— John V. Rabbits, "Fight the Good Fight"

Been around Sable Island and watched the horses there graze on the long grass and trot down the sandy shores, the wind fluttering their manes and tails. Been south around the heel of Nova Scotia into the Bay of Fundy and farther south into the Gulf of Maine, into the waters of the United States of America, where the coastal villages' wooden piers, docks, and moored ships were the same as those back home in Newfoundland. Been past icebergs that were the size of the foothills near Cape Ray. Heck, been as far east as the Grande Banks to where all you could see with a spyglass on the horizon was rolling blue in every single direction. But it was in 1941, as war raged across the Atlantic, that *The Waddler* forged home through heavy seas to St. John's, her hold brimming with cod. And as the gales of November stalked us like a blue shark on a sea lion's backside, Uncle Patty shared a tale from the Great War that drastically altered the course of my life.

"Pay heed, lad," said Patty. He held the wheel true, gazing out into the night. "The German horde was fearless that day at the Battle of Arras. They poured up from their holes. Chargin' through the rain and mist and smoke as if one-horned demons *crawlin'* from the abyss. Sent by Lucifer himself. Only us Blue Puttees held 'em back. Wave after wave stormed our line. Their rifles tipped with bayonets. Bloodlust in their eyes, screaming *Angriff!*"

"What's it mean?" I cringed as soon as the words left my mouth: to Patty interruptions might as well have been hurled insults.

He scowled at me and cleared his throat. "It means *attack*, lad. Our Vickers cut them down. Mortars exploded, yet still the Huns charged." Sheet rain pelted the wheelhouse's windows. A gust buffeted *The Waddler's* hull, and she swayed as she rose from a trough atop a roller to an ocean of undulating darkness. Patty pulled long and hard on his briar pipe, the smouldering tobacco illuming his grey whiskers and crooked nose. He was silent a moment before he exhaled a thick smoke that crawled up around his wool toque and hit the tobacco stain on the wooden ceiling. "No time to be scared. Get you killed on a field of combat it will."

Patty placed his briar down, and hunching over the wheel, he peered out the window. His eyes narrowed, then he clenched his jaw. "*Hang on, lad.*" I lunged and clutched the steel handrail, bracing myself for a ride just as the ship's bow began to rise. Patty stared straight ahead. The brass plotters and chart slid off the table, skidded across the floor, and struck the rear wall. Patty's briar fell next and rolled to my feet. Then a mighty gust hit the starboard hull, rocking the ship to and fro, as she ascended a monster wave.

Patty's wiry frame was unbudging—his legs were rooted like oak trees. The wheel shimmied, and his forearms bulged as he held it true. White water sprayed across the deck and pounded the windows, another gust hit the hull, then a loose line lashed the wheelhouse. Patty growled over the chaos and shoved the throttle forward. The diesel's pistons fired like a salvo as *The Waddler* struggled to meet the demand.

I thought of the tales of lost ship and crew swallowed by the Atlantic. I tightened my grip on the rail, a panicky feeling shivering through my body. With the angle of the bow, we would have gazed at celestial bodies if it were a cloudless night. It felt like we were riding heavenward without the possibility of ever reaching it. Rain machine-gunned the bow windows, a foot from Patty's face. I readied myself for them to implode, for glass shards to slice and gouge our flesh, and for our blood to paint the inside of the wheelhouse. As the wave thrust the ship back in an easterly direction, my guts churned and my heart began firing in my chest like the diesel's pistons, as if wanting to break free of my body. I shut my eyes, gritted my teeth, and panted as if I had already plunged into the frigid ocean and joined the lost.

As *The Waddler* was on the verge of flipping ass over teakettle, as I envisioned us stuck inside the wheelhouse while the ship sunk into the fathoms, the bow began to dip. And it was then I realized we had crested the monster. I opened my eyes. Patty stood steadfast, chest heaving. We descended into a wide trough.

"Bloody rogue wave," said Patty, his voice firm. "Ya'll right, lad?"

"I'm well," I squeaked. My ability to compose myself was not nearly as developed as Patty's, nor at that time did I believe it ever would be. I released the rail and opened and closed my hands a few times to loosen them up. Patty's posture relaxed, yet his eyes remained like full moons, unmoving from the ocean before us. "Pass me my briar," he said.

I stooped and picked up the briar at my feet and tottered over to Patty. He released one hand from the ship's wheel, and with the nonchalance I admired, he grabbed the briar and took a *long* pull from the still smouldering tobacco. *The Waddler* steadily resumed her rhythmic rise and fall, the nor'easter's wind swaying her a wee bit. When I returned from tying off the loose line, Patty took out his knife from the sheath on his hip and carved a nick on the wheel beside the eleven others: one for every time he felt he had been close to meeting his maker. It was the third nick since I had been fishing with him.

"Where was I? Ah, yes. A quagmire of mud, blood, and souls. But the order came and the Blue Puttees obeyed. Climbed from the trenches we'd called home for a month. Stepped over bodies. Pushed on by hollers from our chums, our piper, and visions of glory. *By God*, we charged." He bowed his head, and gave it a wag and tapped his briar against the ship's wheel and seemed to dwell a moment. "I saw what no creature of God should."

I thought of the photos I had seen: the twisted bodies with their rictus grins, seemingly petrified in some act—charging or fleeing—and the miles of mud pocked craters; gapping trenches and shorn tree trunks; and barbed wire stitched across the land.

"Was there gas?"

"No gas. Cannons. Blood. Bullets. And Iron. On that April mornin' in 1917. Five hundred men—sons, brothers, fathers, charged the German line and ran along the duckboards. Some shot, some blown up, others drowned in mud and blood. Only a handful made 'er back. Your father led the men—fearless—and fell that day. He made it farther than any soldier … the road to freedom is paved in blood, lad. Some of it ours. *Remember that*. Our family's given *enough* to the British Empire."

Patty blamed my mother's, his sister's, death on the war as well: he believed the grief from losing my father had snuffed out her innocent life. To me my mother was only a memory—long brown hair, woollen shirt and white blouse, hanging linen on the clothesline, humming songs. Nothing more. And all I had of my father was a sole photograph of him in uniform before he sailed to Europe, and the stories told by Patty. Still, my parents' deaths clung to me like wood smoke to a wool sweater—the very fibre—always present in every scrap, voyage, and challenge. I tasted my tears before I was aware that I was crying. It was too dark for them to be seen, I figured, so I just let them run. A sombre silence then fell between us. As I stared out into the night and listened to the sheet rain and *The Waddler's* hull crash on the waves, I wondered if the same feelings were stirring in him. Patty's vigilant eyes roved the ocean. He had rambled about war, bits and pieces, but neither in such detail nor when clean from the ale and spirits. Why had he chosen then to tell the story—perhaps the wolfpacks sinking ships off the coast? Perhaps all the men enlisting to go fight the Axis of Evil had triggered it, or maybe he simply felt it time a son learned of bravery from a father no longer alive to teach.

As we continued home through the night, the ocean soothed and the winds softened and Patty told stories about romance and sea monsters, and in-between the stories he would load his briar, strike a match, and puff till it glowed. They were stories he had told a hundred times, stories I relished and that never lost their appeal. And come the blue of early morn, we sighted the beacon from Fort Amherst Lighthouse, signalling *The Waddler* and her crew had arrived home safely once again.

In the harbour, large hulls jutted from the ocean like looming icebergs with names like *Britannia, Gibraltar,* and *Norfolk,* and I could smell rusty steel and fresh paint too. I had never seen that much tonnage in one place. There were merchant ships, preparing for the risky crossing of the Atlantic to bring vital cargo to Britain, and American destroyers and frigates. Ships I had sighted for years, wishing I was aboard, headed for a foreign port and adventure. The American army base at St. John's, the naval base at Argentia, and the air force base at Stephenville had all sprung up in a matter of weeks, lifting Newfoundland from poor to flush in under a year, and giving the impression the U.S. was at war, even though it had not yet officially made the declaration.

Throughout the morning, with gulls circling over the smell of cod guts and diving at scraps tossed into the ocean, we unloaded our catch. I listened to the sailors on the pier talking about Nazi coups across Europe and North Africa and places I had never heard of before. Come noon, I was scrubbing the deck when a British merchant sailor climbed atop a crate on the pier as if it was a podium. He waved his arms and called out until a group of a dozen or so sailors and fishermen formed around him, then he began to speak. I leaned the deck brush against the wheelhouse, climbed over the gunwale, and leapt onto the pier and strolled over to listen. The men around the crate were silent, looking up at him as if his words had become images and those images were being stamped into their eyes.

"... and the RAF has staved off the brunt of the Luftwaffe in The Battle for Britain," he said. "But bombs continue to rain down and raze whole city blocks of London. Killing men, women and children. If Great Britain falls, North America is sure to fall." When he finished, the men bombarded him with so many questions that I could not make out single one. The sailor hopped down to confer with them.

Gazing east, I recalled hearing the story of the Spanish town Guernica on the BBC. I pictured the Luftwaffe's fighter planes and bombers emerging from the ashen clouds over the harbour, the fighters strafing St. John's streets, and people running, wailing, and screaming. The bombers dropped their payloads on homes and shops. Everything I had known for years turning to fiery rubble and death.

A holler from Patty jostled me back to reality. He was standing on the *The Waddler's* deck. He gestured toward the brush and shook his head, his smoking briar hanging from his mouth. Nodding, I raised my hand and gave a wave. As I hurried back to finish cleaning the ship, the possibility of a Nazi invasion seemed more real to me than ever. And it was right then that I made the decision to enlist, to drive the Huns back into their holes—back to Lucifer himself.

After we finished up in the harbour, I headed to the Church Lads' Brigade Armoury, home of The Blue Puttees. It was situated on Harvey Road in the military district of St. John's. Ever since I moved from Cape Ray to St. John's to live with Patty, I had watched parades there, listening to the pipe-band's drums and skirling bagpipes. I marched up to the armoury's white façade and towers, and arrived at its heavy-wooden double door, under the concrete archway. I knocked four times, each time louder than the previous.

A moment passed, and then a latch unlocked and one side of the door opened. A young clerk greeted me, shook my hand, and asked me my business. After I informed him that I wanted to enlist, he led me into the armoury. There was a large indoor parade square with two large rectangles, one inside the other, their lines painted in white. On the other side of the armoury there was a door on which had FIRING RANGE stencilled in red. I could see flags on the right-hand side: British, French, American. Laughter echoed from somewhere. The clerk led me to the right and then left down a long hallway past one solid wooden door. He stopped at the second and rapped quickly twice, the echo resounding in the hallway. From inside a gruff voice ordered us to enter. The clerk smiled and winked, and headed back down the hallway. I entered the door and was greeted by the smell of stale tobacco smoke, and a hint of aftershave. A grizzled officer sat across a barren desk with a shellacked top, his hands steepled in front of him. He ran me up and down with his grey eyes as I shut the door and walked toward him. The hefty cluster of metals on his olive green uniform would have made a good anchor. On the walls, there were photos of ships and servicemen, and a bookcase was set against the wall behind him. And against it leaned a flag pole with what looked to be a furled Union Jack on the end.

"I want to enlist in Her Majesty's army, sir," I said, hands clasped behind my back.

"Have a seat." He gestured to a wooden chair in front of the desk. "Why do you want to join?"

"Do my part to *stop* the Nazis," I said, sitting down.

He grinned as he opened his desk drawer and removed some papers, which he then slid toward me. "We can use more brave young men such as yourself. What's your name?"

"Thomas Paul Gerard."

He paused, nodded a few times, then tapped his pen on the desk. "You'll make a fine Blue Puttee in the Royal Newfoundland Regiment, my boy. Call me Officer Muldar." He extended a hand and we shook, and I felt thick calluses, the kind only earned by hard work.

"How tall are you, lad?"

"Five foot eleven," I said. "Half inch taller with my boots on."

His right eyebrow rose and he jotted down my height on the enlistment papers. "How many stone?"

I thought of the fish scales on the pier. "Eleven, five. Give or take."

"Schooling?" he asked, continuing to fill out the papers.

"My uncle taught me arithmetic, how to read charts, maps," I said, and gestured to his bookshelf. "And books, I read lots of books and newspapers too."

"Way of living?"

"Fisherman, on my uncle's boat, *The Waddler*."

"You're blood to Patrick Burl," he said. And I was unsure from the way he said it if he had meant it as a question, so I simply gave a quick yes. He grunted and rubbed his chin, and handed me the ink pen and stabbed his finger at three lines on the paper, told me to sign my name.

I scrawled my signature on the lines without reading a single typed word.

He scooped the papers up and slipped them back into the drawer as naturally as I baited hooks on the long line. "You begin basic training tomorrow. Be back here at 0600 hours, get your kit in order."

"Yes, Officer Muldar." I saluted.

"The Huns will not subjugate the world with men such as you committed to the fight for freedom," he said, his voice taking on a Churchill tone. "Say goodbye to your family and friends. And your lady if you have one." He rested his fingers on the desktop and leaned forward. His grey eyes widened, alight. "It may be sometime before you return."

We shook hands again. I stood, pushed the chair against the desk, and went to the door. As I turned the doorknob, he spoke softly: "Your father would be proud."

I paused, my back to him, feeling the cool brass of the doorknob in my fingers. "Sir, my father died at the Battle of Arras."

"I know, son. A tough man and brave soldier."

When I exited the armoury, I felt raw yet relieved, as if I had cleaned and dressed a wound on my body. I wondered how my father and Patty had felt back in 1916 after they enlisted. I strode along Harvey Road into a light snowfall falling from a darkening sky, toward my own frontline, not in Europe or Africa, but right there in St. John's.

It took a moment for my eyes to adjust to the smoky haze, as thick as harbour fog, in Cale's Beer Parlour. A haven for townies, loggers, and all those who earned a living from the ocean. Everyone fresh off the dole with war-effort pay to spend. The Tabernacle Trio, a folk band I had heard many a time, was playing an unfamiliar tune and the patrons followed along with claps, stomps, and drunken tongues:

"Gone to Russia to find some oil, in a fountain he will boil ... round, round, Hitler's grave ... round, round, we go ..."

I spotted my uncle through the smoke and revelry at his corner table, his back to the wall. Gesticulating, briar in hand, he was in the midst of narrating a tale to a spellbound audience. Wending around some jigging patrons, I made my way to his table. Patty had yet to see me when he thudded his mug down, sloshing ale. He then lifted his arms above his head: "... it came like Neptune's spear risin' from the depths to take *The Waddler* and her crew to a watery grave—*a two hundred footer. A wall of water. A leviathan, gentleman."* He snatched his mug, took a deep swig, and hunched forward, gazing around the table. "Didn't bat an eye. My nephew and I rode—"

"Stop your *balderdash*," yelled a man from two tables over. "Just like the time you caught a mermaid on your long line. Everyone knows you're full of—"

"Only thing everyone knows, Ben, is your tart's ways when you're gone to sea," hollered Patty, springing out of his chair. Francine was a French lass that had been attached to Ben, ever since her father had gone missing while lobstering in his skiff a few years before. She was half Ben's age and true to Patty's claim as I am sure a good many in Cale's could attest.

I cringed. The parlour silenced and the band stopped playing. When words lashed in Cale's, fisticuffs usually followed. If provoked, Patty could dole out a brute licking. And neither man nor nature stood much of a chance against him in a clash. Watched him bite a man's ear clean off once, wash it down with ale as the poor fella writhed and moaned on the floor, covering his remaining ear, hoping Patty was not hankering for dessert, no doubt. A chair's feet scraped on the wooden floor. Someone coughed. All eyes were fixed on Patty.

Ben slammed his mug down, knocking over the drinks at his table. His three chums were unsure of what they should do, their heads swivelling around, trying to read the mood of the patrons, perhaps the way their favour was leaning. As he pumped his fist at Patty, Ben's eyes bulged out of his red, veiny face. "I've known you for twenty years, Patty. But you *ever* talk about Francine that way again … and …" He jumped up, kicked over his chair, and stormed across the parlour and out the door. A man shut it behind him. It was silent for a moment, then The Tabernacle Trio started up with a song. Patrons clashed mugs; they stomped and clapped as if nothing had happened.

"There you are, lad," said Patty. He leaned over and pulled out a chair for me, hops and pipe tobacco strong on his breath. Patty's chum, John, greeted me with a stiff handshake. Patty poured me a mug of ale.

"Where the hell you been?" asked Patty.

"C.L.B. Armoury." I sat down.

"Whatcha doin' there?" He took a swig.

The Trio's fiddler screeched to life, so I leaned toward him and spoke loudly: "I enlisted. Begin basic training tomorrow at 0600—"

Patty's mouth burst open, showering the table and John with ale. "Are you bloody daft? Tell me you're jokin'?"

"Jesus almighty, Patty. Couldn't you've aimed that spout down?" said John. He shook his head, mopping his cheek with a sleeve.

"Let me speak to my nephew," said Patty, ignoring the grievance. "Family affairs, you see."

John got up, and headed to the bar, mug in hand.

Patty's eyes narrowed. And I pretended not to notice while he studied me. He held his briar in his fingertips, chewing on the stem, as he did when mulling something over. "I promised your mother I'd look after you as she lay on her deathbed."

The vibrations in the floorboards made it impossible to tell if I was shaking or not. "It's *my* choice," I said. "I'm a man. I made the decision and I'll live with it."

"That's the problem, Tommy. You got a scurvy dog's chance at living *if* you go over there. All those books got you hungry for adventure. You don't need to go to war. We can head farther out. We can try new fishin' grounds. Even return to the Banks," he said excitedly. "In a few years you'll own half *The Waddler*. We'll be partners. Me and you—or you and me. We'll bring catches home so heavy they'll call us the scourge of the Atlantic. Regular old pirates we'll be."

"I'm going." I clenched my jaw as I had seen Patty do all my life.

"We've been over this and over it. It's not our war."

"It is our war. It's every British son and daughter's war. It's every free man, woman, and child's war. The Nazi's aren't going to leave. U-boats are sinking ships in our waters." I waved at the ceiling. "Next the Luftwaffe will be dropping bombs."

He hammered the table, his face fierce. He pointed the stem of his briar at me. "One more soldier won't make a difference."

"What about the two who left here in 1916—did they make a difference? You talk proudly of your service, yet try to frighten me from doing my part."

"I should've known you'd be as bold and unpredictable as your father. Almost the same words came from his mouth. And I bit. Hook, line, and sinker. Watched the crows steal your father's eyes and flies lay eggs in the holes. Watched your mother fade to nothin'." He shook his head back and forth and he sighed a great sigh, as if he had just seen a great tragedy. We both picked up our mugs and began to drink, only feet away yet fathoms apart.

Over the last year, he had to have known there was a yearning in me. Young, bold, proud, determined. The questions I would ask sailors, or others we knew who had enlisted. It was then I understood why he had decided to tell me the tale of Arras. Because he knew I was on the cusp of enlisting. He could see it. He loved me and wanted to protect me from the atrocities he had experienced, what had killed my father.

We sat silently as John jigged with a buxom lass of ill-repute and the music and merriment carried on around us. Patty was motionless, his briar smokeless at arm's length.

A good time passed before Patty ordered two more flagons of ale. By the time we were into the second one the mood was calmer between us and our tongues began to loosen. We spoke no more of war. Instead, we reminisced about adventure and bravery as we drank late into the night in Cale's smoky and raucous parlour with the rugged men who braved the elements and the women who braved those men.

In the early morning dark, I walked along Harvey Road, blinking sleep from my eyes. A heavy snow was falling, swirling about, and a gale from the harbour whistled along the cobbled streets and narrow laneways, carrying woodsmoke from chimneys and a blare from a ship's horn. The stone homes rose two or three stories on either side of the road, their windowpanes frosty. I imagined people inside wrapped in their quilts and wool blankets, as I had been an hour ago before Patty woke me up and hugged me farewell.

A few minutes along, the armoury's towers appeared through the dark sky and falling snow. As I got closer, I could make out the bagpipes skirling faintly. Then there was a sound behind me, like footsteps crunching softly. When I turned around, I saw only my vanishing tracks on Harvey Road, the road where I first heard the bagpipes to freedom play.

The Test

I was chewing oatmeal as I watched the great white shark torpedo by the cameraman in the shark cage. When the phone in the hallway rang it startled me, only because of how much louder it sounded with my sister and mother still in bed. I'd been expecting the call, so I got off the couch and rushed into the hallway to answer the phone, impressed by my speed.

It was silent, then a boy's voice gave a simple order: "Be at Suicide Island in thirty minutes." A click and dial tone followed, and I hung up. As I tiptoed upstairs to my bedroom, I was bright-eyed-and-bushy-tailed. After all, I'd been waiting my entire life for this chance to prove I was now a man. Eleven long, long years.

After I changed from my Spiderman pyjamas into shorts and a T-shirt, I reconned the upstairs. My mother slept hugging her pillow, which made up for my father, who was on tour with his regiment in Somalia. Next I checked on my sister. She was asleep too, surrounded by her stuffed unicorns. The usual for a Saturday morning in the Grainger household. If my father was home, we would've been getting ready to head out and fish the river for bass or walleye or big old channel cats. Or maybe we'd be driving into Pembroke to shop at the Army Surplus, pick up some cool army shirts with military insignias and sayings like "Death from Above" or "Kicking Butt and Taking Names." Over the previous few years, my father had been away on back-to-back tours in places like Cypress and Bosnia, as had my friends' fathers. Morale was on the decline, my father said the last time he was home, men were going to start burning out. It seemed the older boys had stepped in to fill our fathers' boots, toughening us younger boys up with arm-bars and chokeholds and dares that "made men out of boys."

I padded barefoot downstairs to the back entrance where I tugged on my raggedy pair of Converse that I used as river shoes, then slipped out the screen door to a clear July sky and glowing sunrise. I dashed across the dewy field beside the PMQ, startling a flock of sparrows. I gave chase. By the time I entered the woods my feet were damp. There was a chorus of birds and insects and the smell of pine and raw earth hung in the air. Smells I'd known since I first ran those woods, soldiering with my buddies, barefoot sometimes, toy gun with me all the time. Remembering what the older boys had said about conserving energy for The Test, I slowed to a march on the shady path leading to Suicide Island. I pictured myself walking home in a few hours. A man's victory walk, shoulders back—proud, steady, and heroic—like my father's whenever he returned home from work.

Twenty minutes later, I could hear the roar and crash of the Petawawa River in the distance and my heart began to race and hands tremble. At that moment, there was the first hint of doubt. I thought of the tales of drunken soldiers who'd stumbled along the same path and leapt into the river and drowned, and of the teenagers from Pembroke, goofing around, whose car accidentally rolled into the Mackey's Rapids and sunk with them inside. Rumour was the undercurrents had washed them down river close to the island, and both wreck and bodies were still at the bottom. But mostly, I thought of Donnie Chenski. He was a ten-year-old from the base's south side who'd drowned two years before while trying to pass The Test. No one knew he'd drowned for three days, because the other boys who'd been involved had been too frightened to come forward. It was only after one boy's little sister told her mother what had happened that the MPs were notified and the search began. Donnie's body was never recovered. I recalled overhearing my mother's words to my father after the search had been called off: "The poor family must be devastated knowing the river just swallowed him up like that."

When I arrived at the top of the thirty-foot bank, the launching area overlooking Suicide Island, I gazed down at the swift and roiling Petawawa River. It was darker than the water of Otter Lake where my grandparents lived. Images of bloated bodies with empty eye sockets and skeletons tangled in weeds bobbed up from somewhere in my mind, like deadheads in the river. I took a deep breath, opening and clenching my hands, trying to calm the tremble that had only gotten worse. The island was off to the left a ways, allowing challengers some leeway, as the strength of the current would sweep even the strongest swimmer downriver. It was so small that I thought it would be tough to hit with a stone. It was so small I'd spent many nights laying in my bed while staring at my G.I. Joe figures, wondering how a little hump in the river could mean so much to so many, but always falling asleep before I'd found an answer. Right in the middle of the island, next to a barren and stunted tree, sat a large pile of rocks which I knew carried great meaning—the Suicide Pile—and next to it, a painted turtle basked in the sun.

I smacked my gums, worried about the bitter taste I'd been warned of for years. All the older boys I looked up to said it might start to creep in during times like that, the taste known by deserters and chickenshits—the taste of cowardice.

There were footsteps behind me and I turned. My buddy Petey was walking toward me on the path, and when he waved and smiled, the tremble began to calm. Petey had that way about him, whether we were about to charge the Frenchy's fort or chat up Sara and Rebecca at the roller rink or outside the movie theatre after a Saturday matinee. We'd been buddies since before I could remember. I knew this because his mother had photos that I couldn't remember being taken.

"Knew you'd show, buddy," said Petey.

We high-fived like we always did when we first met and before we separated.

"It doesn't look that bad," I said, nodding at the island.

Petey stepped to the edge of the bank and kicked the earth and caused a small avalanche, sending up a large dust cloud.

"Nay, if Greg and Steve made it we got this all day. We're not going down with Donnie."

A bird chirruped loudly from the treetops and flew out over the river in big loops. A branch cracked and ferns rustled. Petey and I locked eyes for a second, then Chet burst from the woods followed by the towering figure of Miles. Their faces were smeared with green camo stick and they were dressed head-to-toe in green camo fatigues. They were both thirteen-years-old. Older boys needed to be present to witness younger boys challenge The Test, and then spread word of the results. I figured Chet and Miles had been spying on us in hopes we would take off so Chet could brand us as chickenshits. Chet *was* known as Chet the Tyrant.

As they marched toward us, Chet yanked off his green cap, exposing a light re-growth of red hair and his birthmark, which was shaped like a kidney bean and took up half his forehead. "I was sure you twerps were going to be chickenshits," he said, flapping his arms. "*Bwack, bwack, bwack.*"

"Told you they'd be here," said Miles in his boomy voice.

I smiled. Miles winked. Although the two of us had never played marbles or soldiered together, we lived in the same PMQ block and saw each other daily. Our fathers talked often, swapping fishing holes or borrowing tools. Stuff like that. And last summer he and my fourteen-year-old cousin, Kylie, who visited every summer, hung around more than my father and mother had liked.

"What's wrong with you, Dylan? You're pale and shaking." Chet waved a hand at me. "Ah, he's chickenshit." He nodded as if he had me all figured out. He wiggled his pinkie finger in the air. Wiggled it like worm. "Don't worry, nothing's gonna bite it off. It's just a little wriggler. A perch wouldn't even look twice."

The older boys roared with laughter, bouncing and shoving each other. They pounded each other's fists, like every one did after they scored a goal or watched a hero in the latest action flick wipe out a gang of scumbags. I felt my guts squirming. I didn't like it. Was I chickenshit? Was I fooling myself thinking I could make the swim—there and back?

"Least he hasn't whizzed himself," said Petey.

Chet's lips tightened, his kidney bean darkening. He balled his fists, eyeballing Petey. Everyone at school had heard the rumour: Chet supposedly whizzed himself right before The Test a few years back. Something he denied.

"Alright, smartass," barked Chet, puffing out his chest. "Our fathers need to pass a test to join the Airborne so we need to pass this test." He jabbed his finger toward the island. "You need to get down the bank and swim across to Suicide Island. You need to pick up a rock, put it on the Suicide Pile, then swim back and climb the bank. If you screw up," he grinned wickedly, "well, you know what happens."

I knew as did every other base brat in Petawawa, on both the north and south side. If we failed to cross and put our stones on the Suicide Pile, we would be branded as chickenshits. We would never get to join the Airborne and would be trampled into the mud for the rest of our lives. And what about the girls? They would simply pass by us at the roller rink, ignore us at the matinees. We would probably end up as cooks, peeling spuds or scrubbing pots and pans, far from the foreign lands and adventures our fathers talked of often. All our hopes for the future crushed like June bugs on a windshield. Or, we might end up down at the bottom of the river with Donnie.

Petey huffed, as if it was no big deal, and patted my shoulder. "We know. We'll make it. *Right, Dyl?*"

"Yeah, yeah, we're gonna make it. No problem," I said, my voice cracking. I swallowed harder than I would've liked to and wiped sweat from my brow, wondering if the other boys could hear my heart pounding. I'd make it? It wasn't impossible. Other boys had. I'd swam farther at different spots along the river, other spots where the current was just as swift and strong. But never *this* length with such a current. Then Petey pulled off his Incredible Hulk shirt and kicked off his shoes. I did the same. I felt as if I was facing a firing squad: tense and ready for a round between the eyes. Our shadows were unmoving before us on the five feet or so of bank. I squinted at the heat waves dancing above the island's shore, the sun tingling my bare skin. The painted turtle boogied into the river and disappeared. I couldn't recall ever seeing a turtle move so quickly. It was as if it sensed what was about to happen and didn't want any part of the action. I was unsure how long we stayed like that before Petey said, "Don't *stop* for anything. Hit the water and go."

I managed only a grunt.

Miles said, "You can do it," and gave us thumbs up.

Chet the Tyrant had picked up a gnarly stick and was wielding it like a club as if ready to chase us off the edge. "*Go. Go. Go,*" he screamed, his kidney bean a dark purple.

Petey glanced at me. We both nodded, and then we stepped to the edge of the bank and jumped and hit the dirt and began to slide down. I shut my eyes and mouth as dust enveloped us. I heard Miles holler, "Don't let your legs get caught in the undertow," before we splashed into the river.

The current pulled, battered, and whirled me. I fought to the surface, took a deep breath. Cheers and claps erupted from behind us. When I spotted him, Petey was already swimming toward the island.

The current was sweeping us down river. I breaststroked after him, thinking that was it—pass or fail.

With every stroke and kick, the doubt I'd been feeling faded more and more and I felt strong following Petey's bobbing head, the splashes from his feet and arms. If the soldiers' bloated bodies and skeletons existed, if Donnie Chenski and the teenagers in the wreck were down below—all wanting company—they would have to wait, because I swam faster than I did at the beach races, even faster than the ones at the rec centre. I was that great white I'd watched earlier torpedoing through the ocean. Only I wasn't hunting seals or spooking a cameraman in a shark cage, I was hunting my destiny and a strike would change my life forever.

As we reached the halfway point, Petey's head and limbs disappeared. I slowed my breaststroke to a crawl and scanned the water, the current carrying me a long. Nothing. He was gone. I turned and tried to yell at Chet and Miles, who were both watching from atop the bank. Water sloshed into my nose and mouth. I gagged and spun around. The island was close. Even though my arms and legs were weakening, I knew I could make it.

I thought of Petey somewhere under the surface. Thought of the time our snow fort collapsed on me, and how Petey, who'd been outside, dug me out, just as I'd begun to panic and gasp for air, terrified that I was going to suffocate.

I cried out, took a deep breath and a last look at the sun, then dove under. It was dark and turbulent, my eyes slowly adjusting to the dim underworld of the river. The bottom was lost in a forest of tall stringy weeds swaying around in the current. A monster pike flashed past, its cold, dark eye fixing on me momentarily before it shot into the weeds. I swam forward and down, my lungs beginning to throb, eyes swell, the roar of the Mackey's rumbling in my skull. And then off to my left, a flash of white in the forest of green. A limp arm. Petey's arm. I grabbed it frantically with both of my hands just as my mouth burst open, the air from my lungs expelling in a torrent of bubbles. I fought toward the surface, hauling Petey to a sunlight that had never looked so distant and strange.

When I breached the surface, I rolled onto my back and struggled to lift Petey's slippery body up so his head was out of the river. Weeds had entangled around his neck as if they'd been attempting to choke and bind him to the bottom. We'd been swept down to where the river opened up wider and the current was weaker. A large rock jutted out from the shore into the water. Petey and I had fished off it in the spring, eyeing up the challenge we knew would come that summer.

I started a lopsided backstroke, like a wounded frog I'd once seen. And I remembered how that frog's legs had twitched before it was snatched by a fish. My arms and legs burned as I headed to the shore. Chet and Miles were shouting. When my shoulder struck rock, I reached back with my right arm, struggling to hold Petey in my left, and slowly inched my way onto the rugged surface, which was warm against my body. I sat upright and dragged Petey out of the river by his wrists, his arms stretched out behind him. He was pasty white, his eyes closed, lips a bluish tinge.

The shouting was growing louder. Chet and Miles ran toward us along the narrow trail atop the bank. Petey would die for sure, if I didn't do something. I removed the weeds from his neck. I tilted his head back and pinched his nose and blew three times into his mouth, then placed one shaky hand over the other and pumped down on the center of his chest. C.P.R. just as I'd learned from the lifeguards at the rec. centre. I repeated the steps again, and while I pumped his chest a third time, water erupted from his mouth and he jerked to life as if he'd been shocked by electricity. He choked and retched. Water continued to come out of his mouth. I quickly lifted him onto his side, and patted his back. He started to gasp for air, his arms flopping about.

Chet and Miles were now running on the lower portion of the bank. Petey rolled onto his back, his chest heaving as if some bone inside was trying to blow out.

"*Petey, Petey*, you're alright," I said. "Take it easy."

Petey raised a hand to block the sun. "We didn't make it?" he said quietly.

I looked at the island as the older boys arrived.

"You guys alright," said Miles. He leaned over us, his hands on knees, breathing heavily.

"You two are screw-ups. With capital S's," said Chet, his kidney bean black from exertion. We were all breathing heavily.

"I screwed it up for us," said Petey. He stared at me wide-eyed. I'd never seen him look so weak and upset.

"Everyone's gonna know you two failed," said Chet. "Big *time* screw-ups."

Miles stood straight up and turned to Chet. "No they didn't. They both made it."

"What are you talking about? They—"

"They made it farther than you did," boomed Miles.

Chet the Tyrant vanished for a brief moment. His face took on a look of fear and uncertainty. He glanced quickly at us and then back to Miles. The two stared at each other. It was silent, except for the river and the distant drone of a plane. Then Chet nodded and he and Miles reached down, grabbed Petey's arms, and helped him to his feet. Petey wrapped his arms around his body, shivering, and looked at the island.

As we walked off the rock together, our shadows fell behind us.

Longest Serenade

The city was speaking to him tonight, through the ancestors deep within him. They had awakened from their slumber early that morning as Benny John rode to work. They only spoke like they did today on rare occasions and tonight was definitely one of those, his final performance of the summer. A rare occasion indeed. A once a year event.

Ten years running now, ten straight years of performing, the ancestors' voices whispering at first and then growing louder and louder until it was as if they were chanting right in his ears. And the streets of Victoria, well, the streets were like limbs he had adopted and now cared for as he cared for his feet and legs, arms and hands, his ears and eyes and nose, like his heart and mind and spirit. He was a part of the city; the city was a part of him.

Benny wheeled his Suzuki moped down the narrow alley toward the street where his venue had been for the last four months, and for those four months last year. He closed his eyes. The steel-cased fans on the bricks thrummed, networks of rusty fire escapes jittered, and moths and other winged insects thumped stubbornly against the plastic light covers. You see, Benny had a gift, he could take sounds and make beauty, even sounds no one cared for. It was a gift from the Creator said an Elder once during a sweat ceremony.

With all the sounds in the alley, he heard a tribal drum beat and rattles and he thought of the Cowichan Valley. Oh, how long it had been since he visited his reserve, feasting on sockeye and elk, dancing in the longhouse while those drummers beat those big drums. He could *always* feel those big drums if he tried hard enough.

When he passed a large blue dumpster, he caught a funky smell in the air. He did not mind. Because his cowboy boots smelled too, especially by the end of summer after he had been busking three times a week from the first of May till the last day of August. Which was today. And he dealt with funky smelling clothes at Brown's Used Goods where he had been working for years. Clothes worn by the dying that reeked of mothballs, and medication which sweats out of the pores and into the fabric, Mr. Brown had said. He told Benny to always wash that stuff with extra detergent.

Three men rounded the corner into the alley. They were young, buffed-up, and hairdoed-up. Except for slightly different heights they looked pretty much the same. The tallest one in the middle had a large doughy face, like uncooked bannock. He was flinging his arms about and barking out a story to his buddies. Benny was certain he had never seen them before tonight, because he never forgot a face, just like he never forgot a voice or a tune. Not wanting to bump into them, Benny hugged the dumpsters on the right side. When the shortest of the three, who was on the left, backhanded Doughy Face's shoulder and pointed at Benny, they all looked. Doughy Face spoke: "Why don't you take your guitar and sing us a song. Or did you just rip it off."

They started laughing, snickering, and shoving one another. Benny was unsure if they were joshing with him. But he had been around enough drunken people to know they were good and pickled.

"Look at the mug on him," said the one on the right, pointing at Benny.

"Must've fallen out of the ugly tree and hit every branch on the way down, fucking mongrel," said Doughy Face.

"Crooked eye and all. Got to be a retard," said the one on the left. "And who the fuck rides a moped?"

Benny did what he usually did in these cases, just wheeled past them without even so much as a flinch. He had heard words like those too many times to count over the years: words that used to pierce him like a flaming arrow in the heart. But nowadays when he heard them, Benny let them pass right through. And then the three were behind him, still carrying on, whacking one another's backs, as if congratulating for a job well done. They were talking about lap dances at the Red Lion and G-strings and shots of tequila when Benny exited the alley heading toward his venue.

He had picked the spot because of the green city bench and garbage can and magic bricks, and also the pub and nightclub and oyster bar a half block up. Not to mention the sliver view of the harbour with the sailboats' masts and the Pacific Ocean that stretched on and on like a song you never wanted to end. People enjoyed his performances here, the tunes he sang and strummed or finger picked on his Yammy. People always told him they loved his music and one woman even said he looked like a young Leonard Cohen. He had performed for all sorts: the mayor and his wife; Americans, Europeans, and Asians from the cruise ships and even a few Russians who kicked up their feet in a strange dance; there had been NHLers whose names he had forgotten, and even Pamela Anderson twice. But it was the locals he saw nightly who energized him the most, gave him that feeling of belonging. Nigel and Axle. Corbin out for a tour in his wheelchair, building up endurance for his *tour de force* cancer marathon to Tofino, which was always put off until the following summer. And Crystal out in her short dresses and high heels and coils of bracelets, just 'taking in the fresh evening air' and it seemed the early morning air too.

There was no traffic as he crossed the street and bumped the Suzuki up the curb onto the sidewalk. He set it up on the kickstand beside a lamppost covered in posters for night clubs, comedy shows, Tai Chi in the park, and underground DJs and haunted tours of the city. He unlocked the padlock at his waist and unwrapped the chain from his hips. He bent over and slid the chain through the front tire and looped it around the lamppost and locked the padlock. Last year, on a cool summer night in July or August, he could not remember for sure, he had been performing for a large audience when a man dressed all in black edged up to Benny's banana-yellow Norco mountain bike. Conspicuously. The man stood there for a minute, coolly looking back and forth, before he grabbed Benny's Norco by the handlebars and ran it onto the street and leapt on and rode away without even a glance back. No one noticed except Benny—everyone had been too caught up in his performance. He watched it all happen, not even missing a chord.

Benny figured the man in black must have needed a bike something fierce. The Suzuki had come to him within a few days anyhow. He was lucky like that. It seemed the Creator knew just what he needed and provided accordingly. A truck had pulled into the fenced lot behind Brown's where people always dropped goods off. Two men got out and lowered the tailgate. They dumped the Suzuki moped, a rusty BBQ, a set of old Kenwood house speakers, and a fake palm tree (as tall as

Benny) onto the asphalt. Brown sold the Suzuki to Benny on a payment plan: twenty dollars deducted from his bi-weekly cheque for the next year. Brown even threw in the palm tree. It only took a tune-up at a small engine repair shop to get the moped running properly. And now the Suzuki ran better than the man in black did with his Norco.

Benny unslung the black nylon guitar case from his back, unzipped it, and lifted the Yammy out by the neck, feeling the polished mahogany and steel strings in his hand. New strings he had put on today as soon as he got out of bed—his final performance ritual of the summer. He strolled over to the coffee shop's brick wall, dropped the open case at his feet, and nudged it with his boot tip. The top flopped shut so he leaned over and opened it up. If people tossed change from the bench, he wanted them to have an easy time of it. Always thoughtful. Plus he hated to hear coins tinkle on the sidewalk.

The brick wall added something to his acoustics that he had never heard before last spring. Maybe it was the type of brick or maybe their age. It was as if a hundred little Yammies belted out onto the street in every direction. A busker's paradise, like his city.

Benny slung the Yammy over his shoulder. He stood there taking it all in. Ocean blowing up from the harbour, cleaning away the exhaust. A group of young people passed by, chatting away excitedly, out on the town. They were followed by a well-dressed middle-aged couple smiling and holding hands, content without words. Somewhere a club's speakers pounded hip-hop. He leaned back against the wall holding the Yammy's neck, its body resting on his boot tip. If he listened long and hard enough—extracted what he needed—he knew he could create a beautiful musical masterpiece with all the sounds of the city. He took what no one else paid attention to, what no one wanted, and made it special. Like he did at Brown's with all the clothes he washed, folded, and hung out on the racks for sale; like all the old stoves and fridges he scrubbed and cleaned so Brown could sell them in Vancouver; like the furniture he repaired (what he could) and polished and set on display. And like the stickers on the discarded suitcases he heated up with the hair dryer and peeled off to stick on the Yammy so it resembled the city's lampposts. At that he lifted the Yammy up until she was out of the shadow. He studied her. Cologne, Montreal, Barbados, Paris, Shanghai, Toronto, New York, Rome, and Parry Sound, Ontario: Home of Bobby Orr. There were other buskers—Chris who played country on a twelve string, and the violinist who wore a Darth Vader costume—but he was the only one whose instrument had been decorated with city stickers. It made him feel different to have them on there, not the kind of different he had been told he was, but some other kind he could not quite explain.

Still a few hours or so before the big rush, after the bars and clubs shut down for the night, when people headed home or stumbled to parties or strolled to their boats or wherever else they went. Some would stop; others just keep walking by as if they did not care for live music. But that was alright.

Benny lifted the Yammy and slung the strap over his shoulder, clamped a bar chord, and strummed all six strings, getting an electric feeling up his arm. He smiled for as long as the chord reverberated in the night. Across the road a few people on the sidewalk stopped, turned their heads in search of the cause. Benny took a deep breath and let it out. He slipped a red bread tag from the pocket of his Levis. His arms and hands and fingers came alive to run the gamut of chords, each time he hit the strings harder and faster, priming, getting ready to go. She was chanting tonight—something powerful—as if she knew tonight was the last night of August, the final performance until next May.

He started to play Spirit of the West's "Home for a Rest," a song he had picked up off the radio a few years back. After he finished a long set, he took a moment, taking in the city—distant laughter, thumping bass, people walking by, and in a single lit window above the flower shop across the street, there was the silhouette of a person.

He began to play a tune he picked up last week, but forgot the name of. He closed his eyes. The electric feeling crawled up his arm and spread through his body as the big Yammy and little Yammies resonated on the street. When he ended the song, he opened his eyes. There was an audience of four in front of him. Two middle-aged couples he had never seen before. They had smiles on their faces, eyes alight, as if they truly digged his music. He started up with "Fortunate Son" to keep the momentum going.

Benny's audience grew and shrank and grew and shrank as he continued with his set. Some people stopped briefly, others stopped for a few songs. He finished the eighth song with a tune from The Band. Everyone clapped and someone whistled. People tossed handfuls of change into the case. An older man with a ponytail, who looked like Jesus, stepped forward and dropped a folded bill on top of the change. The audience drifted away until only a young man and woman remained.

Benny stuck the bread tag in his lips and went over to the Suzuki. He lifted his helmet from the moped basket and hung it on the handlebars, then unzipped the bike bag inside the basket, where he kept three Red Bull. He could squeeze in three and three served him well for a night of busking. It helped him get to where he needed to be. He had long ago given up the hootch.

"How long you been playing for?" said the young man, his voice excited. He could not be more than twenty, shaggy brown hair, pimples on his cheeks, black hooded sweater, as if he had just gotten out of bed twenty minutes ago and did not care what anyone thought.

"Since I was five," said Benny.

Five the man mouthed, and looked to the woman. She had very straight blonde hair down to her shoulders, glasses with dark blue frames.

"That's insane," said the young man. "Did you hear that?" He pointed at Benny, eyes still on the young woman.

She had a phone in her hand, maybe texting or surfing or playing a game. Benny popped the tab on a Red Bull, hearing a fizz, and chugged a long drink.

"I've been taking lessons for two years. Don't even sound close to that," said the young man. He turned to Benny. "You're friggin awesome. How'd you learn, tab or chords?"

"From the radio."

"As in you listen to it and play it?"

"Yup," Benny said. It was how he learned, intently listening to the radio, eyes closed, snagging every bit of sound blaring from the speakers. He could pick out a guitar that was out of tune by the tiniest, could tell when a guitarist's timing was off too. From those Kenwood speakers, the radio played all day in the back room of Brown's. Classic Rock 101 from Vancouver: *The best of the 60s, 70s, and 80s.* Benny listened at coffee time and lunch time and all the times in-between as he separated, washed, and priced clothes. Brown did not want him working up front, said he did a 'fine job processing goods in the back and it would be foolish for him to have Benny anywhere else but where he was.' So at work he learned song after song for his stock, for the four big months of the year when he opened up and shared with the city.

The young man was shaking his head, staring at the Yammy. He started whispering cities—New York, Halifax, Paris or maybe Parry Sound.

"Probably a musical genius like Mozart or Lady Gaga," said the young woman, still fixed on her phone. "We stopped Matt, now let's go. They're waiting for us. We already missed dinner and now we're hours late. Dad's going to be pissed. Sherry already thinks we hate her guts for being a home wrecker."

"Older sisters are nags." Matt gave Benny a thumb up. "Keep on rocking."

Benny flashed the peace symbol and chugged the rest of the Red Bull.

Matt and his sister walked toward Douglas Street, but then Matt turned and jogged back to Benny, pulling out a chain wallet from his back pocket. He slipped out a fiver and dropped it in the case and said, "Amazing, thank you." His sister was standing a ways up the street, still doing whatever on her phone.

Benny tossed the empty can into the garbage and whirled around in a circle, strumming a few chords, keeping his fingers loose. There was no one left. The breeze coming up from the harbour carried voices and laughter. His music no longer kept the audience glued to the venue. Usually how it went, or so it seemed. He stepped to the edge of the curb and looked toward Douglas Street. Matt and his sister were out of sight, a crosswalk was flashing and beeping, taxis sped through the intersection, people were crossing, and scattered groups were coming toward him. He zipped up the bag as a police car pulled up to the curb directly in front of the bench. The window was down. Officer Holden, who Benny had known for years, sat in the driver seat. Holden and his wife would stop and listen to Benny play once and awhile. The passenger seat was empty. Holden's salt and pepper hair was shorter than Benny remembered, and he had a moustache now.

"Hey, Benny, nice night to be outside," he said, hanging his arm out of the window. "Did you pick up your busker license yet?"

"It's my last night tonight." Benny gave his head a quick tilt to the brick wall. "Won't play out on the street again until next spring."

"If you busk in the city of Victoria you need a license or you will be fined. You know this. And I write enough tickets, Benny, for all sorts of foolish things. I don't want to write you one again. But if I don't another officer will."

Holden shook his head and craned his neck to look in the rear-view mirror, then turned to scan the other side of the street. Benny went up to the window. On the dash there was a computer screen lit up and a radio beeping and squawking. A black shotgun was secured to the console. A Plexiglas barrier separated the front seats from the back and he could smell industrial cleaner, like the kind he used at Brown's to clean the doors handles and counters and bathroom after the store closed up for the day.

"How's your wife?" Benny asked.

"She's fine," he said, turning down the radio. He let out a long sigh. "We're expecting a baby girl this month."

"Next summer you can bring the family for a performance, should be at the same venue."

"You never know. Look, Benny I'm not going to write you a ticket tonight, but please get a busker licence next spring or you'll end up paying more in fines than you make and that's not using your noodle," he said, tapping a finger against his temple. "Besides, you don't want to get so many fines you end up in the hoosegow. Not the place you want to land again. Try putting a note on the fridge, that's what I do." He thrummed his fingers on the car door and said, "Have a good night," and drove away in the direction of the harbour. Benny watched him leave, thinking there was no need for a note: he had four tickets in his bike bag, and he did not like to waste paper.

"Hey, how's my man doing tonight?"

Before Benny turned around, he knew from the voice it was Nigel. He was strolling toward Benny, Axle leading the way, straining on a shiny chain leash, paws scrambling on the sidewalk as if it was a sheet of ice. He was a little brown critter with a flat face and short hair, always huffing away, sort of like Nigel.

"Played for awhile tonight, just waiting for the rush, gonna happen soon here," said Benny. He slid the guitar to his back, knelt down to pet Axle, who jumped up and pawed his arms, slobbering on his sleeve.

Nigel bent over and scratched Axle's head. "Get your mug off Benny," he said, lifting him up. Axle's legs scurried in the air. "The Yammy fits you nice like an Italian tailored suit. Snazzy. All those stickers you put on add character, like scars, and you know the ladies dig scars. Right, my man."

Benny slid the Yammy to his chest and drummed the body. Then he rushed his hand along the neck, rasping the steel strings. "Been told the sound carries up to Douglas and *all* the way down to the promenade and parliament building. Even during the rush."

Nigel did his lip thing as if he was kissing the air and lowered Axle to the sidewalk. Axle scurried over to the garbage can and began poking his nose around. "You play like you're possessed by voodoo witchy. You do, people everywhere hear. You're a modern day minstrel right here in the capital. Always be cool, my man, put out the love and you get it back. Might not feel like it sometimes, Benny, but it's gonna come one day in a big way. Karma and righteousness make legends outta common men. And remember, when you retire the Yammy I'll set you up with a fine Canadian made music making machine, do it on a payment plan, like last time. No need to walk out of the store with a guitar ever again."

"Could land in the hoosegow," said Benny, feeling his face warm.

"Right, o, and the hoosegow's no place for an icon of the city. You know what I mean, my man."

Man, words streamed out of Nigel musical-like, like a long song that Benny could always rely on to lift him up whether he needed it or not. Axle cocked a leg at the garbage can and let go with his own stream.

"Enough talk, let me hear some thunder from that lightning of yours," said Nigel.

Benny was all warmed-up now, Red Bulled-up. And from inside the lightning came alive, out to his arms and hands, working the Yammy, that thunder Nigel had asked for pealing across the city in the form of "Blister in the Sun." Nigel sat on the bench. Axle was at his feet, head cocked, tongue hanging out.

Come the second chorus, people had gathered around in a half-circle and surely his tunes carried something powerful—even spiritual— tonight. Heads bobbed along and feet tapped on the sidewalk. A black man who had puffy black hair held a black woman with puffier hair. They swayed together as if they were a single willow branch moving in a light breeze. When the song ended, Benny started up with another. Nigel dropped a bill into the case and he and Axle left. The guy with the ponytail returned and sat on the bench and began air-drumming with his fingers.

A group of young people arrived. They were wearing white robes and layers of colourful beaded necklaces. Benny saw it all but it passed right through him, like those words from the men in the alley earlier, like light through a crystal, like those crystals Starla, his third foster mother, hung from above the eastern windows in her house and from the rear-view in her rusty Volkswagen van—morning sun scintillating through in a thousand places. He was like one of those crystals then, taking everything in and letting it pass right on through him. And even those thoughts passed right through him. There was no control needed, no sensation in his fingers; they clamped chords and strummed strings as if they were acting on their own, maybe possessed by voodoo witchy. The only way he knew he was still playing was from the sound of the big Yammy and the little Yammies and the smiling faces. All sorts of people began to show up. They looked unique when they first arrived and then similar as they blended in with the others. In the window across the street there were now two black shapes uniting and parting, really fast. He felt sweat trickling down his forehead and so he whipped his head side to side, hurling sweat onto the sidewalk. When he finished the song, there were claps, yips, and a finger whistle—shrill like those bald eagles he had watched from the banks of the Cowichan River, circling in the blue overhead as he fished the blue below with his cousins, listening to his uncle share tales of the trickster, who turned people and dogs to stone.

Benny launched into another song written by the guy who wore the little round glasses who was shot dead in New York outside his apartment by the guy with the book. Coins glinted and flashed as they rained into the case. None of it mattered. He would have played if there was no one gathered around. He would have played if it were only the city's bricks and glass, alcoves and alleys, homeless and drug addicts. He would have played for free. He would have played if it were only for the ghosts that he passed by in the alleys. Benny was a pumping heart that would continue to beat long after the body had went to sleep.

After he hit the final chord, he bowed at the waist, the sweat on his forehead dripping onto the sidewalk. He stayed that way for a moment and then removed the Yammy and leaned it against the brick wall. As the audience began to leave, they tossed more coins and a few bills fluttered into the case. A single red rose wrapped in plastic, the kind the street vendors sold, lay inside on a pile of change. Benny had not seen who dropped it in there. He stepped over to the Suzuki and put his jacket on the seat. He reached into the bag for another Red Bull. Taxis were driving up and down the street, some occupied, others vacant. Benny stepped off the sidewalk, and when he heard the crosswalk on Douglas beeping, he turned and looked. There were people crossing the intersection and heavy bass thumped from a dark SUV as it passed by. He unzipped his leather vest so his Pink Floyd T-shirt could breathe.

He put another Red Bull back in three long gulps. There were people passing by on the sidewalk, but everyone had left the venue. He underhanded the empty can into the garbage and walked over to the brick wall and lifted the Yammy by the neck and slung it over his shoulder.

"Was that you I heard playing ten minutes ago?" A woman with long curly black hair stood there, seeming to have paused just to ask him the question. Four other women about the same age had stopped farther along, chatting away, as if they had stopped just for her.

"I was playing a few minutes ago," said Benny. "Where'd you hear it?"

"On the main street. Outside a bar waiting for drunk chicks," she said, gesturing at the four women behind her.

"Jess, let's go," said a woman in a squeaky voice. "They'll all be there and I want to get in."

"There's a limit. It'll be full soon," said another. The other two moved slowly away. One dug around in her black purse the size of a small suitcase, and the other yelled something about cover charge into her phone.

"You play classic rock? Lightfoot, BTO, Hendrix—all that." She was ignoring her friends. She had the softest brown eyes and longest eyelashes and a few freckles on her nose. Her voice was a smooth song, effortless, natural, as if she spoke like that all the time. And maybe she did.

Benny nodded.

She turned to her friends. "I'll meet you there."

"Come on, everyone will be there, and if it sucks we can leave. We won't be stuck there," said Squeaky Voice. Her friends were drifting away, not paying any attention.

"I'll catch up. Listen for your phone," said Jess. "I'll call when I'm on my way."

"Are you serious?" She shooed a hand at Benny and gave a serious face. "A street person over DJ Loki? He's only here for the weekend. It's the only chance we'll get to see him."

Jess winked at Benny and waved the others off. The girl with the purse marched back to Squeaky Voice and latched onto her arm and began pulling her along. The other one was still on her phone walking backwards, unbothered.

"Please hurry," said Squeaky Voice. "Don't repeat last summer, keep your phone on." Then she went along freely with the others toward the harbour. Benny felt a chill, his arms goose-bump. It was time to play. He interlocked his fingers and cracked his knuckles and whipped his head side to side until his neck cracked.

Jess sat down on the bench, crossed her legs, and strummed an air guitar. Benny grinned and looked down at the tip of his boot and scuffed it on the sidewalk. He figured she had that free-spirited, "do the dishes tomorrow, don't worry be happy, love and peace and happiness Woodstock" way about her. Benny bent over and picked up the rose from inside the case and stepped over to the bench and handed it to Jess. She lifted the rose to her nose and shut her eyes, holding it there as if dreaming of the most beautiful place in the world. He backed up to the wall, strumming a few chords, and when the magic bricks reflected the one-hundred little Yammies, he stopped dead and let go with Hendrix's "The Wind Cries Mary."

Halfway through the song a young couple stopped, and by the time he finished, a dozen or so people were gathered around. Next he played Lightfoot. Some others passing by expressed interest but like Jess's friends they were herded along by others who it seemed had other plans. But that did not upset or even bother Benny. For him it was not about reaching everyone and hoping they liked his music—it was about reaching those who did and he knew he was different but he followed his heart and treated people rightly even when they treated him badly. It was about feeling bliss and hoping others felt it too.

An older couple held each other, as the black couple did earlier, as hundreds of couples had done while listening to Benny's music. And he wondered if any of them knew how similar their holding was and he felt a pang then and thought how long it had been since someone had held him. A light flickered off to his left. Corbin rolled up—one handed—in his wheelchair, waving a lit lighter back and forth. A bald man wearing a Hawaiian-T sparked his lighter and started waving it. Two more lighters flamed.

A rift opened up in the audience and Benny saw the shoulder of a man beside Jess. People shifted and the rift closed. The audience swelled around him as people who had been walking along the sidewalk stopped. The city was shutting down and the final rush was underway. More lighters sparked until there were flames waving everywhere like a rock concert right at Benny's venue and the big Yammy and the hundred little Yammies seemed louder now as he was the sole source of music.

When the rift opened again, Benny got a look at the man next to Jess. He had short brown hair and wore a blue polo-T, collar popped. He was resting one leg over his knee and had his arm slung over the back of the bench as if he was a son of the city. He leaned closely to Jess's ear and said something and put his hand out in front of her and snapped his fingers like the hypnotist Benny had seen get a man to howl like a wolf. And he thought the man beside Jess looked like one of those men who pulled into the back of Brown's in a BMW or Mercedes, and climbed out and popped the trunk to fling garbage bag after garbage bag of old wealthy people clothes onto the asphalt. Their dead father's or mother's or sometimes both. And they always seemed to want leave quickly, as if they had dumped an unwanted passenger who they did not want catching up to them.

As the minutes passed, the audience dwindled. Soon all that remained were four people standing in front of him, the silhouettes in the window, and right next to each other on the bench Jess and the Hypnotist, his arm wrapped around her shoulder and his hand hanging like a rattle-snake's head ready to strike. If Benny had not talked to Jess when she first arrived, he would have guessed them for a couple. The group of four left. Only Benny and Jess and the Hypnotist remained. A taxi passed by and then a police car that Benny thought Holden was driving. The Hypnotist was whispering to Jess as if everything around them was nonexistent.

Benny shook his head. He kicked the flap of the case shut and readjusted the Yammy. He tuned the strings, and then he closed his eyes and started to play. He thought of the friends and family that he loved and the ones he had lost. He thought of the joys and triumphs and hurts and disasters he had felt over the years. He thought of the endless ribbon of joyfully smiling faces and those people who he knew his music had touched in some deep way. Then he went inside of himself and called upon his spirit. From Bryan Adams to Cockburn, from 54-40 to Tragically Hip and on and on and on. And with his eyes shut, his fingers alive, he exorcised all those sins that he had learned of at residential school—anger, lust, greed, gluttony, sloth, pride, and covetousness. He let go of the other words that had been drilled into him, words like Amen, Holy Ghost, Blaspheme, Jesus Christ, and *Devil tongue*. Rivers of sweat ran into his eyes, stinging, reminding him of the tears he had not cried since the shrunken, drug-riddled face of his mother appeared on the evening news, joining all those other faces of Vancouver's Missing Women. And she had been so beautiful before, before the wounds she carried had festered and poisoned. Benny dropped the bread clip and fingered Spanish style, what he used on those nights when he needed to be closed up after feeling the pain from all that had been stolen from him over the years. He went deeper inside of himself, and when his fingertips throbbed, he went deeper. Time became lost to Benny, as he played the longest serenade.

When the Yammy's top string broke and lashed Benny's cheek, he opened his eyes. The sky was salmon-coloured. A dark curtain had been closed in the window above the flower shop. The bench was vacant, sidewalk empty. Seagulls cried overhead and somewhere a dump truck's hydraulics hummed. A poster blew past. Benny's shirt clung to him, the sweat-soaked cotton cooling on his skin. He took his sleeve and wiped his eyes and turned the Yammy around to his back and bent over and lifted the case, the money pooling in the centre. He carried it over to the bench and plunked it down. A line of rose petals blew by the tips of his boots. The rose he had given Jess lay on the sidewalk, one petal remaining on the end of its broken stem, the plastic loose and flapping. Then the wind tore the petal loose. As it passed by Benny's boots, he almost reached for it but he did not and then it was gone.

"Been a long night," said a man hoarsely, sitting to the right of Benny.

Before he turned, the smell of gin and tequila hit Benny. It was Doughy Face from earlier in the alley, his hair wild, a large red goose-egg under his left eye. "You alright?" asked Benny.

He huffed and said, "They left me. You believe that?" He was slurring his words. "I'm going back. I'm going back to fix them up real good." His upper body swayed in little circular motions like a harbour buoy. The neck of his shirt had been torn.

"Can I get you a taxi?" asked Benny.

Doughy Face turned suddenly and reached his left hand into the case and grabbed a handful of money. Benny clutched his hand above the wrist with both of his hands. Doughy Face glared at him and tried to tug free but failed, tried again, then a third time.

There was a click right before a flash of steel in Doughy Face's other hand arced toward Benny and struck him in the center of the chest. Benny tried to let it pass through him like he had been doing for years with the memories and teasing. He let the hand holding the money go.

Doughy Face jumped off the bench, knocked Benny's helmet off the moped handlebars, and bolted across the street. Change tinkled on the asphalt.

Benny touched his fingertips to his chest. He lifted them up. They were covered in thick, dark blood. His hand trembled uncontrollably, dropped onto his lap. He heard the ancestors chanting, the beating of eagle wings. He shut his eyes and fell sideways onto the case.

I could hear my heart beating.

I could hear everyone's heart.

I could hear the human noise we sat there making,

not one of us moving, not even when the room went dark.

-Raymond Carver, "What we talk about when we talk about love."

About the Author

Shawn Gale writes on Canada's West Coast. He is a graduate of Fraser Valley Writers' School and Humber College's School for Writers, where he earned a Letter of Distinction. His stories have appeared in periodicals and anthologies in Canada and the United States.

He is currently a student at the University of Wisconsin-Madison.

Printed in the United States
By Bookmasters